Constantine's black winged brows drew down very slightly. "So, you haven't come here to tell me?"

Cold swept through me, my gut twisting and making me feel even more ill. I put a hand on the back of the uncomfortable couch, steadying myself, because he couldn't know. He couldn't. I'd told no one. It was my perfect little secret, and that's how I'd wanted it to stay.

"Tell you?" I tried to sound as innocent as possible, to let my expression show nothing but polite inquiry. "Tell you what?"

His inky brows twitched as he looked down on me from his great height, his beautiful face as expressive as a mountainside. "That you're pregnant, of course."

Rival Billionaire Tycoons

Dark-hearted brothers set on vengeance!

Valentin and Constantine Silvera were once each other's only support under their cruel father's rule. But the circumstances of their childhood drove an irreparable wedge between them and ultimately drove Valentin to escape in the only way he could imagine: by faking his own death.

Now Valentin is back, and he's on a mission to reclaim his inheritance. But neither of these hard-hearted billionaires are backing down! It will take the women they are destined for to show them there's more to life than power and control...and perhaps even to reunite them.

Read Valentin's story in
A Diamond for My Forbidden Bride

Read Constantine's story in
Stolen for My Spanish Scandal

Both available now!

Jackie Ashenden

STOLEN FOR MY SPANISH SCANDAL

H HARLEQUIN
PRESENTS

HARLEQUIN®
PRESENTS™

Recycling programs for this product may not exist in your area.

ISBN-13: 978-1-335-73864-6

Stolen for My Spanish Scandal

Copyright © 2022 by Jackie Ashenden

For questions and comments about the quality of this book, please contact us at CustomerService@Harlequin.com.

Harlequin Enterprises ULC
22 Adelaide St. West, 41st Floor
Toronto, Ontario M5H 4E3, Canada
www.Harlequin.com

Printed in U.S.A.

Jackie Ashenden writes dark, emotional stories with alpha heroes who've just gotten the world to their liking only to have it blown apart by their kick-ass heroines. She lives in Auckland, New Zealand, with her husband, the inimitable Dr. Jax, two kids and two rats. When she's not torturing alpha males and their gutsy heroines, she can be found drinking chocolate martinis, reading anything she can lay her hands on, wasting time on social media or being forced to go mountain biking with her husband. To keep up-to-date with Jackie's new releases and other news, sign up to her newsletter at jackieashenden.com.

Books by Jackie Ashenden

Harlequin Presents

The Italian's Final Redemption
The World's Most Notorious Greek
The Innocent Carrying His Legacy
The Wedding Night They Never Had
The Innocent's One-Night Proposal

Pregnant Princesses

Pregnant by the Wrong Prince

Rival Billionaire Tycoons

A Diamond for My Forbidden Bride

Visit the Author Profile page
at Harlequin.com for more titles.

Carry on, my wayward son...

CHAPTER ONE

Jenny

I ONLY WANTED one last glimpse of him, the man I once loved.

The man I now hated with every breath in my body.

Constantine Silvera. My stepbrother.

It wasn't the best choice of occasions—his father's wake—but I didn't want to go near him or talk to him. I only wanted to see him and from a safe distance.

Domingo Silvera, once CEO of Silver Inc, one of Europe's most powerful conglomerates, was being farewelled at the Silvera family's ostentatious Madrid mansion, and I'd sent Constantine a short, impersonal email offering him my condolences and promising I'd be there.

But I wasn't there for Domingo. I didn't care about Domingo. My mother had married him when I was nine and then promptly sent me to boarding school in England, so I'd never had much contact with him. Which was a good thing since he was a very difficult man.

No, the man I wanted to see was his son. One last time before I cut him out of my life.

It was probably a bad idea, and my poor heart had been through enough the past three months, but I needed to say goodbye. Even if it wasn't actually to him. Even if it was only for myself.

So here I was, hiding behind a column in the white marble-covered ballroom, hoping I'd be lost in the crowd of dignitaries trying to catch a glimpse of him.

Not that it was difficult to catch a glimpse of him when he towered above everyone else in the room and drew every eye.

They called him cold, merciless, ruthless, and maybe in business he was. But he'd never been that way with me. Initially he'd been reserved and distant, yet I'd come to know the man beneath the ice. A kind, caring man.

At least until I'd moved to London permanently four years ago, and then, for some reason, he'd cut off all contact with me.

All contact except once, three months ago, when I'd discovered something else about him: there was fire deep in his soul, a fire that only I knew about.

A fire I'd discovered the night I'd seduced him.

At his engagement party.

My gaze drifted to the woman at his side, tall and blonde and poised. Olivia Wintergreen, CEO of Wintergreen Diamonds, an old and very successful jewel company. She wore a fitted black dress and her pale lovely face was composed. She was everything I was not.

She was also his fiancée.

A business arrangement, I'd heard through the grapevine, since certainly Con himself hadn't told me. An old friend of the Silvera family, chosen as a potential wife and mother for his heirs. He didn't love her, so the gossip columns reported, but she had good genes and came from a good family and, as CEO of a large company, she was his match in every way.

And I was…not.

I was short and round and not at all beautiful. I was not a CEO. I worked with the homeless in a shelter in London, much to my mother's disgust, and I had no poise to speak of.

I was not his match, as he'd told me that night, after he'd had me on the grass near the rosebushes in the garden outside. And I never would be.

The memory made my throat close with pain, but I ignored it. Normally I tried to be optimistic, to look on the bright side of things, but after that night in the garden looking on the bright side had been more difficult. And I was tired of pain. Fury was so much better, so I reached for that instead. Not that I was angry with Olivia Wintergreen, or jealous. How could you be jealous when your own personal god wanted to marry another goddess?

No, there was only one person I was furious with, and he stood in the middle of the room, tall and arrogant and icier than any glacier.

He was in a perfectly tailored, horrifically expensive black suit that clung to his wide shoulders and hugged his broad, muscular chest, emphasising his narrow waist and long, powerful legs. He looked like an emperor from ancient Rome, as if he should be wearing a laurel wreath, a snowy white toga and a cloak of imperial purple.

His face was as familiar to me as my own, and it made the ache inside me deepen. There were his imperious cheekbones, his straight nose, his hard and yet somehow sensual mouth. His inky hair was cut very short, and his eyes were even blacker, and he projected the sharp, ruthless menace of an apex predator.

He was beautiful. So beautiful.

People were afraid of him. They thought he was just as merciless and as ruthless as he appeared, and twice as cold. Detached from all emotion. But they hadn't seen him tuck a blanket around me when I'd fallen asleep on the chair in his office, or frown in concern over a nest of sparrow chicks I'd rescued and demanded help with, or give one of his very rare laughs when I told him a funny story.

He was only like that with me, and he had been right from the day I'd first met him, when I'd first arrived at the mansion at nine years old. And he hadn't been detached that night in the garden, when he'd dragged me down onto the grass. Somehow I'd unlocked his passion and fire had burst out of him...

But I couldn't think about that night. That way only lay heartache, and it wasn't the lesson I wanted to learn from my relationship with him.

I was going to take some of the ice he gave to other people and place it in my own heart, so I'd never be so stupid again as to fall in love with a man I could never have.

Constantine's black gaze raked the ballroom as if he

was looking for something, or someone, and I wanted to shrink back behind my column, to stay safe out of his sight. Except another part of me, a harder part, wanted to show him that he hadn't destroyed me with the harsh words he'd said to me that night. That I was stronger than he thought.

That I hated him with every part of me.

So I stood my ground, and lifted my chin, and waited for the Sword of Damocles to fall.

And it did.

His gaze found me in the crowd, as I knew it would, and all the breath left my body. But I didn't go cold—I never went cold when Constantine looked at me—I went hot, like a fire blazing high.

He was already statue-still and his expression betrayed nothing. I'd always been able to read him, and yet tonight I had no idea what he was thinking.

His attention raked over me and for a moment or two I trembled. With heat. With desire. With desperate hunger.

Then he looked away, dismissing me as if I was dirt he'd wiped off his shoe.

Tears of rage prickled behind my eyes. Rage at him and at myself for coming here, for thinking I could bear one last glimpse of him without my heart breaking all over again.

I was stupid. I was so stupid.

Blinking fiercely, I fought back my tears and turned away.

I'd had my last glimpse. I'd said goodbye. Now it was time to leave, and the sooner I got out of here the better.

I threaded my way through the crowd to the closest door and stepped out into the relative quiet of the white marble hall.

I was starting to feel a bit sick, since I'd skipped dinner, and the emotion clogging my throat didn't help. So I was distracted, too wound up in raging at Constantine, to notice a man in a black uniform suddenly appear at the end of the corridor.

'Miss Grey?' he asked politely as I approached.

I recognised him. He was one of Constantine's security staff. 'Yes?'

'If you would follow me, please? Mr Silvera has instructed that you are to wait for him in the small study.'

I blinked in surprise. Constantine wanted to talk to me? Why? What could he possibly want to say to me that he hadn't said that night in the garden? Not that I wanted to hear him say anything at all. In fact, the very last thing in the world I wanted to do was to talk to him.

'I'm sorry.' I tried to be polite, even though I felt anything but. 'I have a plane to catch. Please tell Mr Silvera that he—'

'I'm afraid Mr Silvera insists.' The man gave me an apologetic look. 'Just following orders, miss.'

Shock rippled through me. Constantine was *insisting*? But...why? Hadn't he said everything he needed to three months ago? Things such as, 'No, I don't love you. What a preposterous idea'. And, 'Did your mother put you up to this?'. And, 'If you think I'm going to marry you, you're sadly mistaken. You have no money and have no power. You have nothing I want. Your looks might be passable, and you might be good in bed, but sex is not a basis for marriage.' And, 'This was a mistake. And it will *never* happen again.'

Perhaps he'd forgotten to say a few things. Perhaps he hadn't finished tearing my heart to shreds and now he wanted to finish the job.

I didn't want to give him that opportunity, but the way his security man was standing made it obvious that no wasn't going to be an acceptable answer. Which left me with either an undignified struggle or going willingly.

Well, didn't you want him to know how much you hated him? This could be the perfect opportunity.

That was true. The night of his engagement party, after I'd fled the garden, weeping like the stupid child I was, and finally got back home, I'd lain awake, my heart in ruins, allowing fury to fill me. Thinking of all the things I wanted to say to him. Things that would destroy him the way he'd destroyed me.

I'd loved him for so long—since I'd been sixteen—and the way he'd cut me off after I'd moved to London had hurt. And after the passion in the grass, where he'd fallen on me like a starving man falls on a feast, I'd thought that finally, *finally*, he was mine, and the past four years of silence had been an aberration. I hadn't expected his complete and utter rejection. It had come completely out of the blue.

Naive of me. I hadn't even realised it was his engagement party. I'd gone because my mother had told me that Constantine was having a party. He'd wanted me to come and my invitation must have got lost in my inbox. I'd arrived late, not knowing what the occasion was, and gone straight to find him. He'd been out in the garden, alone, and…

Yes, I'd been stupid, and that night he'd shattered me. I'd been too broken to say a word. I'd turned around and run away from him instead.

But things had changed now. It was three months on and I'd found strength in fury, so why shouldn't I give him a taste of his own medicine? Say all the things I'd dreamt of saying to him that night? Perhaps even demand to know why he'd been so distant with me for so long.

None of that would matter at all to him, but it would certainly make me feel better.

Ignoring the clutch of anxiety, I nodded and let myself be led down another corridor and into a small room. As a child, I'd gone to stay at the Silvera mansion every school holiday, and in that time I'd find myself some out-of-the-way place to sit and read peacefully. Away from my mother constantly picking at me.

Usually it was Con's office, but sometimes I'd come in here. It wasn't the most appealing room, though I appreciated the shelves lined with books. However, the couch that sat in front of the fireplace and the two armchairs that flanked it were hard and uncomfortable. The floor was tiled too, and there were no rugs on the floor, no soft surfaces anywhere.

This was a room you showed your enemies into when they came to visit, not your friends.

I'd only taken a couple of steps into the room when the security man shut the door behind me. And I heard the lock click.

Then all the lights went out.

For a second all I could do was stand there, frozen in shock. From outside I could hear shouts, and a few screams, and fear caught at me. I had no idea what was going on, and now I was…locked in.

My heartbeat thumped as I turned and tried the door handle, just as someone on the other side turned it.

And pushed the door open.

I stumbled back, gasping, then the lights flickered on again, illuminating the man standing in the doorway, filling it completely with his height and breadth.

Constantine.

His cold black eyes found mine instantly, the way they had downstairs, and some expression I didn't understand shifted in them. Then he stepped through the doorway and shut the door behind him, trapping me in the room with him.

My heart thumped harder, all my earlier bravado leaking away as if it had never been. My knees had gone weak and my stomach twisted. What a pathetic mess I was. Nothing like his cool, poised fiancée.

No wonder he didn't want you. You should have listened to your mother.

I shoved that thought away and tried to swallow, tried to find my voice, but my throat was so dry I couldn't speak. While Constantine stood in front of the closed door, staring at me, studying me like a scientist examining a flaw in an otherwise perfect experiment.

'Wh-what happened?' I managed to force out. 'Why did the lights go out?'

'Nothing you need concern yourself with.' His voice

was icy and deep, the lilting Spanish accent I'd always loved colouring the words. He took a step towards me. 'I'm glad you're here.'

He was? He didn't look glad. He looked cold and forbidding, all trace of the man I'd come to know and love gone.

I desperately wanted to say all the words I'd been fantasising about saying for the past three months, to tear him to pieces with my anger. But all the words had vanished from my head and all I wanted to do was cry.

Because even now I missed him. Even though he'd broken my heart, I missed him so much.

Pull yourself together, idiot. And don't you dare cry.

I shouldn't, because to do so would give away my anguish, and I wasn't going to do that in front of him. That had been my mistake the last time and I wasn't going to lower my guard again.

But there was a reason why my emotions were all over the place, wasn't there? A very good reason.

'Why are you glad?' I forced out between numb lips.

His black winged brows drew down very slightly. 'So you haven't come here to tell me?'

Cold swept through me, twisting my gut and making me feel even more ill. I put a hand on the back of the uncomfortable couch, steadying myself. Because he couldn't know. He couldn't. I'd told no one. It was my perfect little secret and that was how I'd wanted it to stay.

'Tell you?' I tried to sound as innocent as possible, to let my expression show nothing but polite enquiry. 'Tell you what?'

His inky brows twitched as he looked down on me from his great height, his beautiful face as expressive as a mountainside. 'That you're pregnant, of course.'

Did you really think you could keep it a secret? From him?

I had. I really had. I'd even found a doctor well away from where I lived to confirm it. She wouldn't have told anyone, would she? Weren't doctors supposed to keep their patient's information private?

Fear cut like a knife inside me, combining with hurt and anger and the anxiety of the last three months, plus the lack of food, and making my gut twist again, more violently this time.

I clutched hard to the back of the couch, fighting the nausea, but it was relentless.

I didn't want to be sick in front of him. I'd already humiliated myself enough, hadn't I?

Yet my body didn't seem to think this was a compelling argument. And there was nothing I could do as I stumbled forward a couple of steps and threw up my breakfast all over his expensive handmade leather shoes.

CHAPTER TWO

Constantine

WHEN THE LIGHTS had suddenly gone out downstairs, I'd allowed myself one crystal-clear moment of intense rage. In the darkness no one would see me let out a soundless roar of fury and so I had.

But it was only one moment.

The instant the lights had come back on I was myself again, the way I had to be. Impervious. Detached. Frozen solid all the way through.

Nevertheless, the fury had remained, so when I stepped into that room and my little stepsister threw up all over my shoes I was very tempted to roar again. But that would have been one slip too far, and my control around her already had cracks in it miles deep. So all I did was clench my teeth around the rage until my jaw ached.

I'd known she was here—put me in a dark room anywhere and I'd know the second she stepped into it—and I'd seen her hiding behind a column downstairs in the ballroom. And the instant I had, the frustrating indecision that had dogged me for the past two days, ever since I'd learned of her pregnancy, had coalesced into hard certainty.

My twin brother's not entirely unexpected appearance not fifteen minutes earlier, returned from the dead, had only sealed the deal.

I already knew Valentin was alive. Three months ago I'd had word that he hadn't been killed in a car accident fifteen years earlier, the way we all thought, but was alive and well and CEO of a legitimate company he'd built off the back of various shady enterprises.

I'd known he was going to make a play for Silver Inc, the huge European conglomerate my father and his father before him had built from the ground up, because it was just the kind of thing he *would* do.

I'd even suspected he'd take Olivia, my fiancée. And sure enough, with his usual dramatics, he'd cut the power and spirited her away.

However, I'd been expecting him to make his move during the funeral, not the wake, and no small part of my fury was directed at myself as well as him.

Clearly I'd been complacent.

Now my fiancée had been taken, and while I knew he wouldn't hurt her—Olivia had a considerable history with Valentin—it was a tremendous…inconvenience.

I'd spent a lot of time choosing the right woman and she'd ticked all the boxes. Intelligence, strength, poise, beauty. She was the CEO of a diamond company and had power and influence in her own right.

She was exactly what I wanted, and the best thing about her was that she wasn't anything like Jenny Grey, my little stepsister. My lovely little stepsister. The one woman in the world I could never have.

Except all that had now changed.

Olivia had been taken, and the woman I'd been protecting ever since she was a child—the woman I was still protecting even now, though she'd never know it—was pregnant with my child.

Which made everything very, *very* clear.

For the past four years I'd been holding Jenny at arm's length to keep her safe, both from my father and from me, but one night had ended that. One night and my own lack of control. For two days after I'd found out she was pregnant I'd thought of and discarded various plans that would involve me only peripherally, while at the same time making sure she and the child were safe, yet I hadn't been able to settle on one that would satisfy me.

However, Valentin's little escapade had made the decision for me.

I'd never believed in the inevitability of fate, and yet there was something inevitable this. About Jenny being here, and pregnant, at the same time as Olivia was taken.

So instead of fighting the inevitable, I embraced it.

I'd already given the order to make sure Jenny was shown to this room, since I'd wanted to talk to her about the pregnancy anyway. So the instant the lights went out I fought my way through the confusion to find one of my security team—one who hadn't been compromised by Valentin—and make sure Jenny hadn't got caught up in the panic. Sure enough, confirmation was given that she was in the room I'd set aside for our discussion.

I'd come here with the intention of announcing my plans to her. However, I hadn't expected her to suddenly bend over and throw up on my shoes.

As always, my instinct was to make sure she was all right. Sweep her into my arms and tuck her into bed, keep watch over her. But there was a reason I had to keep myself in check when it came to her, so I stayed rigidly where I was instead.

It did not enhance my mood.

I called one of my house staff to deal with the mess, and ten minutes later everything was clean, I had new shoes and Jenny was sitting bolt-upright in an armchair, a glass of water sitting on the table beside her.

She wore a cheap, chain-store black dress and cheap, chain-store black pumps, and her fingers clutched at the faded black cardigan she'd thrown over the top.

I hated everything about her outfit, since it indicated the dire state of her finances and I hated that too.

Yet again I berated myself for not sending her money over the years, to help her out. Even though I'd been trying to distance myself from her, I could still have helped her out financially.

Not that she would have accepted it. Catherine, her mother, was a gold-digger extraordinaire, and Jenny had always sworn she'd never be like her.

Jenny's dark brown hair was gathered in an untidy bun on the top of her head, with little tendrils falling down around the back of her neck and her small ears.

She was very pale as she released her death grip on

her cardigan and twisted her hands together in her lap instead, looking down at them, her long, dark and surprisingly thick lashes almost brushing her soft round cheeks…

She was soft and round everywhere, her cheeks, her rosebud of a mouth, the lush curves of her breasts and the generous swell of her hips and thighs.

I remembered how soft she was, so hot beneath my hands that night in the garden here, in the grass near the roses. She'd gasped my name and sighed into my ear. She'd been everything I'd imagined her to be, everything I'd fantasised about…

Heat shifted inside me, a thread of dark fire licking around the cracks she'd already made in my armour.

I'd repaired them and had thought I was now proof against the physical desire she always seemed to cause whenever she was in my vicinity, but apparently not.

The fury sitting in my gut coiled and twisted, demanding release, but I ignored it.

I could not feel this heat around her. It was dangerous. It had always been dangerous and that night, when she'd overwhelmed my tenuous control, only proved it.

Keeping myself firmly in check, I elected not to sit, standing by the unlit marble fireplace instead, and looked down at her, waiting for her explanation. I wanted to know why she hadn't come to me when she'd found out she was pregnant and why she was here now, because it wasn't just to farewell my father.

Even Catherine, her mother, my father's erstwhile second wife, whom he'd divorced a few years earlier, hadn't turned up for that.

Not that her reasons mattered.

I already knew what I was going to do about it.

'I'm waiting, Jenny,' I said, trying to curb my impatience. The situation with Valentin needed attending to and people would be waiting for my response. However, I had to secure this situation first. 'I assume you're going to tell me why you are here, if it's not to inform me of your pregnancy.'

Her long, delicate fingers wrung themselves in her lap. 'Does it matter?'

The clear, sweet sound of her voice hit me like a shock, though it shouldn't have. It wasn't as if her voice was unfamiliar to me, not when she had been a fixture in my life for the past twelve years.

She'd mostly been at boarding school in England, but when she hadn't been, she'd been here, small, bright-eyed and full of life. A kitten in the den of a wolf. My father wasn't known for his kindnesses, and even though I knew showing concern was a weakness he'd exploit at any opportunity, I couldn't help the concern I felt for her back then.

She was a child, and very vulnerable, and I knew better than anyone how my father loved to manipulate children.

I'd been nineteen, and working hard for Silver Inc, and even though I'd been travelling a lot on company business, when she'd been there I'd done my best to keep an eye on her.

Then one day I'd come home to find a woman standing in front of me instead of a girl, and everything— every single part of my life—had changed.

But perhaps it was best not to think about that.

'No,' I said, and it didn't matter. I would have found out about her pregnancy anyway, and the end result would have been the same. Olivia was gone, yet she was here, and that made my decision an easy one.

My intention had always been to have a wife, and then children I would guide into adulthood. Heirs to inherit Silver Inc and ensure its future. Olivia had fitted the bill perfectly to produce those children. Mainly because I felt nothing for her except respect.

I didn't love her. I didn't want her. She generated absolutely no heat in me whatsoever.

Which was good. Emotional distance was important and I needed to maintain that, since I had too much of my father in me for safety.

Except my feelings for Jenny had never been distant ones, and marrying her would be a risk, but she was carrying my heir and that had decided me.

She would be my wife, yes, but in name only.

It would have to be that way.

She lifted her head then, her face drawn and pale, her big brown eyes huge and dark. There were black circles beneath them.

Protectiveness shifted inside me again. But feelings were the enemy and they had been for years, and I couldn't fall prey to them now. So I only stared back, cold and hard and detached. Giving her nothing.

Normally, the first thing Jenny did when she saw me was smile, and I'd lived for those smiles once. Small gifts she gave me…little glimmers of light in the darkness.

But there was no warm smile for me today. Her

rounded chin jutted, and an expression of extreme determination hardened her soft features, stealing all her light.

You took that from her.

I shoved the thought away, along with the biting guilt that came with it. I couldn't afford it—or the disappointment that gripped me at the loss of her smile.

I'd never seen this particular expression on her face before, and if I didn't know any better, I'd have said she was angry.

Are you surprised? After what you said to her that night?

The guilt bit deeper.

'Well,' she said crisply. 'Yes, I'm pregnant, and now you know. So, if you don't mind, I'll be going. I'm sorry for Domingo's passing, and you have my condolences, but apart from that I have nothing more to say to you.'

Jenny had always been a joyful little girl, and she'd grown up into a joyful woman. A bright, optimistic woman who always saw the good in people. A soft, compassionate woman.

And, looking at all that softness, it was easy to think that she was soft through and through.

But she was not. I'd caught glimpses of the steel at the heart of her over the years, of a stubbornness that had always been there. Yet she'd never directed it at me before, nor any of the hostility currently bristling in my direction.

Which I deserved.

I remembered that night more clearly than I wanted to. Her in my arms, her face flushed and shining. She'd told me she loved me, and then I'd realised what I'd done, and my anger had escaped no matter how hard I tried to stop it.

I'd been cruel to her. I'd hurt her. Deliberately. I hadn't regretted it then, and while part of me regretted it now, another part didn't. Because it had been for her own good. To get her as far away as possible from me.

Yes, and look how well that worked?

I wasn't a man who made mistakes. But I had three months ago and now the only way forward was to fix it.

'You might not have anything to say to me,' I said. 'However, I have a few things to say to you.'

Her chin rose a fraction higher. 'Is that a fact? And what makes you think I'd be interested in listening to a single thing you have to say?'

Something flickered through me, a spark of an emotion I hadn't felt in a very long time. Curiosity. This wasn't just one of the flashes of spirit she'd shown in the past, this was something more, a glimpse of a strong will that perhaps more than matched my own.

She'd never fought me on anything before, never set her will against mine.

Dangerous.

Yes. Very dangerous. Especially when the beast in me liked a challenge.

On cue, an electric thrill darted down my spine and I had to crush it immediately. I couldn't afford any more temptations, not around her. Not when she'd already undone me so completely three months earlier.

I had to be hard when it came to her. I couldn't allow anything to get through.

'You'll be interested because this concerns your future,' I said, my voice betraying nothing. 'I've known about your pregnancy for the past few days, and I—'

'How did you know?' Jenny interrupted without compunction, a stain of colour appearing on her pale cheeks. Unlike everyone else who knew what was good for them, she'd never been afraid of me. 'Who told you?'

I let her interruption pass. 'I have someone watching you. They informed me of your pregnancy two days ago.'

Her eye went wide, her mouth dropping open. 'You have someone watching me?'

Of course I had. I might have kept my distance from her, but I still kept her protected.

'I've had someone watching you ever since you left Spain. However, I—'

'What? I can't believe this!' Her hands gripped the arms of her chair and she shoved herself out of it, virtually quivering with rage. 'You don't speak to me for four years, and yet—'

'Let me finish,' I ordered icily, my patience thinning no matter how I tried to keep hold of it.

Valentin's little display of amateur dramatics was going to take some time to contain, and containing it was the last thing I wanted to do. I wanted to take care in announcing my decision to Jenny, so it wouldn't come as quite such a shock to her, but I had no time. I had to deal with the mess Valentin had left behind which meant the sooner I told Jenny, the better.

'As I said, I was informed of your pregnancy two days ago. I'm not sure why you didn't come to me straight away, but there's nothing to be done about that now.'

'I didn't because—'

'My circumstances have changed,' I interrupted. 'I have decided I will no longer be marrying Olivia Wintergreen.' I met my stepsister's wide, dark eyes. 'I will be marrying you instead.'

CHAPTER THREE

Jenny

CONSTANTINE STOOD BY the cold marble fireplace, towering above me, his perfect features set in implacable lines, his eyes nothing but black ice.

He couldn't be serious. He couldn't... Could he?

My heart was beating hard behind my ribs, aching at the sight of him despite the shock and fury and hurt. It had been three months since I'd seen him up close and I wanted so much to close the distance between us. Lay a hand on the snowy white cotton of his shirt, feel the warmth of his broad, muscled chest and the faint vibration of his heart.

He might look as hard and icy as a glacier on the outside, but I knew how hot he was beneath it. Like a volcano, there was lava inside him, burning up through cracks in the ice.

Not that you could ever tell, but I knew. I'd always known.

I wish I hadn't. I wish I'd never marched up to him the day I met him and asked him straight out if he would be my friend. He'd looked like he'd needed one and I was an only child. I'd been desperate for a brother.

I'd smiled at him because that was what I did to people who were intimidating, or angry, or people who were sad. A smile could make them soften, forget their anger and cheer up, and Constantine had definitely looked like he'd needed one of those things.

He'd almost smiled in return. I hadn't known then just how rare that was.

He wasn't smiling now, though, and he was certainly nothing like a brother, and I still couldn't get over the shock.

'Wh-what?' I couldn't help stumbling over the word. 'What do you mean, marrying me?'

He gave me the same expressionless look he always did. 'You know what marriage means, Jenny. I shouldn't have to explain it to you.'

I hated it when he spoke like that, his tone cold and superior. But usually he only used it with other people, never with me.

'Don't be an ass, Con,' I said angrily. 'I'm not a child. I know what it means. I just want to know why Olivia suddenly isn't acceptable to you any more. Does she know? Have you told her?'

'Olivia is none of your concern. But as it happens, circumstances with her have changed too.' He glanced down at my stomach. I'd already started to show. 'And she isn't pregnant.'

For a second I thought I saw something hot gleam in his eyes, but it was gone so fast I wondered if I'd imagined it.

'What do you mean, they've changed?' I asked, because he wasn't making any sense. 'Why is—?'

'I do not have time for this.' His black gaze flicked up again, meeting mine. 'I have a situation that needs dealing with.'

'What situation? What's happen—?'

'It's best if you stay here,' he interrupted shortly, and strode with his usual predatory grace to the door. 'A staff member will come for you. We leave within the hour.'

Wait—leave? Leave for where? And why?

I opened my mouth to ask him what he was talking about, but he'd opened the door and stepped through it before I could get a word out. It closed behind him with a sharp click and I was left staring at the white wood in shock.

This was stupid. Did he really expect me to stay here and wait for a staff member? Without any explanation whatsoever? And leaving…? Leaving for where? Why? And why was he being so cold towards me?

Back when I was a child, I'd used to escape into his study with a book and curl up in the armchair he kept in there. The book had been prop, a cover to pretend I was only interested in reading. In reality I'd been waiting for him to turn up so I could talk to him.

I'd been determined to make him if not my brother, then at least my friend.

He'd ignored me at first, but I'd persisted, chatting to him as if I'd known him for years. And gradually, over time, when I talked to him, he'd started to talk back.

At first our conversations had been simple ones,

since I was only nine, and had involved school and friends, and reading and TV, but as I'd got older, our discussions had become more complicated. Books, music, politics, science. Nothing had been off-limits except for two things: the brother he'd lost when he was seventeen, and his father.

I'd never pushed, and by the time I was sixteen he'd felt like my best friend.

Until I moved London and he cut me off without explanation. I'd never understood why.

Now he was offering me marriage, and I still didn't understand why.

I turned from the door and paced over to the chair again, putting a hand to the back of it to steady myself. I still felt sick and confused, and abruptly all I wanted to do was leave.

This whole marriage idea didn't make any sense. The only reason I could think of that he would offer it was for the child's sake.

It wasn't because he loved me.

He'd been clear enough that night three months earlier, when I'd stared up into his beautiful face, seen the remains of passion burning in his eyes, and told him I loved him.

That passion had died instantly, snuffed out like a fire deprived suddenly of oxygen.

He'd ripped himself away from me and looked at me with such betrayal, as if I'd hurt him in some way. 'Well, I don't love you,' he'd told me icily. 'What a preposterous idea.' Then his eyes had narrowed. 'Did your mother put you up to this?'

I'd had no idea what he was talking about, because while my mother had told me about the party, she'd never 'put me up' to doing anything. She might have mentioned a couple of times that if I 'made an effort' I could 'snag' Constantine for myself, but I'd long since stopped listening to her. She might think men were the answer to all life's problems, but I didn't.

I'd tried to tell him that no one had put me up to anything, but he wouldn't listen.

'If you think I'm going to marry you, Jenny,' he'd gone on, even though I hadn't mentioned marriage—even though I hadn't said anything at all. 'You're sadly mistaken. You have nothing I want. Your looks might be passable, and you might be good in bed, but sex is not a basis for marriage.'

He didn't give me time to speak, finishing me off with, 'We must never speak of this again, do you understand? *Never.*'

That was when I'd burst into tears and fled.

My fingers gripped tightly to the back of the chair, more memories of that night filling me. Of arriving in Madrid late, because my flight from England had been late.

'You must have lost your invitation in your inbox,' my mother had said. 'He'll be very upset if you don't go.'

I'd eventually arrived at the Silvera mansion, finding it full of beautiful people, famous actors, politicians, models, the great and powerful—all there to celebrate.

As usual, I'd felt out of place. Because I hadn't been beautiful or great or powerful, and my dress had been from a cheap high street chain. I'd known no one, and I'd spent the first half an hour trying to find Constantine amongst the crowds.

It hadn't been until I'd stepped out into the ornate gardens at the back that I'd found him, standing near the rose garden, half hidden by a tall hedge. He'd been on the phone, talking to someone in Spanish, and he'd sounded…furious. He'd never usually allowed any emotion to show publicly, so the sound of his fury had shocked me. Then he'd cut the call, slipped his phone into his pocket and covered his face with his hands.

That had shocked me too and, unable to see him in distress and not comfort him, I'd moved across the grass to him, reaching to take his hands.

'Jenny…' he'd breathed, as if he'd been waiting all his life for me, and then…

I shoved the rest of the thoughts away. I didn't want to think about what had happened after that, the explosion of passion that had resulted in the small life growing inside me now.

My other hand dropped to my stomach, curling protectively over it.

I should have told him about the baby. I knew that. But discovering that I was pregnant by the man who'd ripped my heart out of my chest and stomped it into a bloody pulp had been shattering. Which wasn't a good enough reason not to inform him, but I'd told myself that keeping it a secret until at least the three-month mark was a good idea. Until, of course, I'd realised that I hadn't wanted to tell him at all.

He was engaged, and had made his feelings about

me very clear, and I hadn't wanted to upend his carefully ordered life with the news that he was going to be a father. He had Olivia, and marriage plans, and it didn't seem fair to derail everything just because he and I had made a mistake.

I'd planned to tell him eventually, but not until my heart felt a little less raw.

My mother, on the other hand, would be thrilled if she knew—'Nothing like a child to keep a man at your side' she'd tell me, even though it hadn't worked with my father, and would likely advise me to take him for everything he had.

But I wasn't like her. I'd never be like her. I didn't want to rely on a man to keep me fed and clothed. I didn't want to end up cynical and bitter. What I wanted was stability and security, two things I'd never had growing up. Oh, yes, and love. I hadn't had that growing up either.

You won't get it with him.

I glanced over at the door.

I'd always thought Con cared for me, but that had been before he'd cut me off for four years without any reason. He'd never explained, so why would I expect anything from him now? And how was that supposed to make me feel stable and secure?

There had been no love in my childhood, no stability and no security, with my mother going from place to place and dragging me with her, looking for men to look after her. She'd never loved any of the men she'd taken up with, she'd only used them. And when she'd got sick of one, she'd found another.

I didn't want that for myself, and I didn't want that for my child. I wanted permanence, a secure home, a job that fulfilled me and a partner who loved me.

I wanted a happy-ever-after, and I knew that wasn't on the table with Con.

Which meant I was going to have to leave.

I'd wait for our child to be born and then, once I'd adjusted to being a mother, I'd contact him again and we would discuss access. But not until then.

In the meantime, I'd get out of here and get back to my hotel, find something to eat and then sleep. My flight back to England the next morning was very early, and I was exhausted.

I moved over to the door and opened it, peering down the corridor.

Silence reigned.

I stepped out of the room and walked towards the stairs, my cheap heels tapping on the unforgiving marble.

At the stairs, another security man in a black uniform appeared. 'Miss Grey?' He glanced down the corridor to the room I'd been in and then back at me. His expression didn't change but it was clear he found my failure to follow orders displeasing. 'Follow me, please.'

I didn't like to be rude, but my anger was still bubbling away inside me, so I gave him a very direct look. 'No, thank you. I was just leaving.'

'Señor Silvera's orders, I'm afraid. There is a volatile situation happening downstairs and I am required to protect you.'

A small, cold shock rippled through me. A 'volatile situation'? What on earth did that mean?

'What kind of—?'

A firm hand gripped my elbow. 'It's nothing to worry about, Miss Grey,' the man said. 'But for your own safety, please follow me.'

Before I knew what was happening I was being hustled down the sweeping marble stairs and towards not the front door, but the back. There appeared to be a large quantity of people milling about in the entranceway, all of them talking loudly.

'What's happening?' I asked, my gut twisting in sudden anxiety. Because it was clear from the looks on the faces of the people that something unexpected and maybe scary had happened. 'Where are we going?'

At the bottom of the stairs, the uniformed staff member urged me down a corridor that led to the back of the house. 'Señor Silvera wants me to tell you that he will be flying you back to England at his own expense.'

Surprise had me almost stumbling over my feet. He was flying me home? That didn't make a lot of sense— not when he'd said something about marrying me. 'But why?' I asked. 'I have a flight booked tomorrow already and a hotel for tonight.'

'He has cancelled your flight and your hotel booking. He thought you'd want to leave tonight. His jet is at your disposal.'

I blinked. We were approaching one of the back doors and I felt as if I'd been caught by a powerful current in the middle of a river and was being borne along helplessly.

This was happening too fast and my brain felt sluggish. I couldn't keep up. Something was warning me, telling me I should pull away and get back to my hotel as fast as I could, but I was tired, and I felt sick, and the thought of being home in my own bed that night was too tempting. Flying in one of Silver Inc's private jets also meant no hassle with Customs or security, no waiting in endless queues or traipsing around airports with heavy luggage. And having to do that felt like too much.

I didn't know why, after telling me he was going to marry me, he was putting me on a plane back to England, but I was too tired to think deeply about it.

Right now, all I wanted was to be home in my tiny, dingy little flat in London.

'Okay.' I tried to retain what dignity I had and not look like a complete mess. 'That sounds…very nice of him.'

The man nodded, and then I was being hurried out through the back of the mansion, where a black car waited. I was bundled into it, and a few minutes later we were driving through the busy Madrid streets.

Some time later we arrived at Silver Inc's private airfield. A jet was already waiting on the Tarmac, the Silver Inc tail livery gleaming in the runway lights.

I was rushed aboard, and I told myself I wasn't disappointed that Constantine wasn't there to say goodbye himself. No, it was a good thing, because now I could relax and put him out of my mind completely. Get back to my job and the plans I'd made for my baby and I.

Because, while I didn't have a partner who loved

me, I could certainly provide the stability and security I craved on my own. I had an analytical brain and I'd already prepared carefully for the baby's arrival.

My maternity leave was all booked, as was my maternity care. I'd have to deal with childcare too, once my maternity leave was over, but I had a bit of time to work that out. I'd been saving every penny I'd earned for the last three months, so I had some savings. I could look after myself and my child, and that was the main thing.

I sank into a seat, the soft leather deliciously comfortable. After the emotional turmoil of the wake it was a welcome relief to be in the silent and warm cocoon of the plane, and I could feel myself relaxing, my heart rate slowing.

We were in the air a few minutes later, with a solicitous flight attendant bringing me a cup of ginger tea and a couple of biscuits that she said would settle my stomach. I didn't ask how she knew I'd been sick, but I drank the tea and ate the biscuits and began to feel a lot better. Dinner was brought to me, too, and it was delicious, and after that had been cleared away I relaxed even further into my seat, the low drone of the engines soothing, making me sleepy.

I'd done what I'd promised myself and I'd seen him. That he'd known about the pregnancy already was distressing, and it made me feel horribly guilty, and all his talk of marriage had been confusing, but I was on my way home now.

It was over and done with. All my secrets were out. I

wouldn't have to see him again until the baby was born, and that was for the best.

I let out a breath. Perhaps I'd close my eyes and rest. Just for a moment.

CHAPTER FOUR

Constantine

BY THE TIME my jet landed at the private airfield just outside Edinburgh I was once more fully in control of myself.

I'd handled the situation in Madrid, suppressing all mention of Valentin's reappearance. I didn't want any part of that getting out, because I didn't want him controlling the narrative, not until the issue of Jenny and her pregnancy had been sorted out.

My lawyers had informed me that, as expected, he'd made a play for control of the company, but I'd instructed them to stonewall him and his team for as long as they could. And, since they were very good lawyers, they could probably stonewall for years.

I didn't need years, however.

My security staff had let me know that Valentin was now headed to the Maldives with Olivia. I'd sent some of my team after them, to ascertain her wellbeing, but I wasn't going to waste time going after her myself. Valentin wouldn't hurt her. They'd once been close friends, years ago, and Olivia was a strong woman. She'd be able to handle him. All that really mattered was that if he was in the middle of the Indian Ocean he wasn't in Europe, making a nuisance of himself, which meant that I could safely suppress the announcement of his return until I was ready.

He wasn't going to take control of this story or of my company. I wouldn't let him. I'd spent years turning myself into my father's yes-man, since that had been the only way I would eventually be able to take control of the company he'd built. Silver Inc was a powerful force in Europe, and Domingo had wanted to take it global since he'd always been attracted to power. But a psychopath—which, clinically, my father had been, no two ways about it—should never have that much control over anything as large as Silver Inc, and someone had had to steer him in order to limit the damage he could do. That someone had been me, though it had meant my being him to a certain extent, so he wouldn't see me as a threat.

However, that was irrelevant.

What was relevant was that if Val thought he could manipulate me with Olivia and undo everything I'd done over the past fifteen years then he could think again.

This was going to go my way. And while I dealt with that, I would also deal with the issue of Jenny.

She hadn't waited for me, as I'd asked, but when the jet had been offered to take her back to England she'd accepted, no doubt thinking she'd be safely deposited back home in London that evening.

Unfortunately for her, that was not going to be the case.

I hadn't had the time I'd wanted to put the idea of marrying me to her, and that had all been Valentin's fault. But I would make time now.

She would come with me, away from the situation in Madrid. Somewhere out of reach of everyone, especially Valentin. Somewhere no one but my most trusted staff knew about, where we would have the peace and quiet I needed to discuss my marriage proposal.

That somewhere was Glen Creag, a bolthole I had in Scotland. A remote estate in the Highlands, where there was nothing but sweeping valleys and mountains and a still, deep loch. There was no internet, no TV. Nothing but the wide-open valley and the sky, and thus no distractions.

The jet I'd put her on earlier had landed about an hour before mine, and my staff had informed me that she was still on board and asleep. I forbade anyone to touch her, and boarded the jet myself to get her.

She was curled up in her seat, fast asleep, her long brown hair coming out of its messy bun and falling down around her shoulders. A curl lay across one soft cheek, and as I bent over her I couldn't resist the temptation to pull it away.

Her hair had felt like silk against my skin that night, as I'd buried my fingers in it, tilting her head back to take her mouth. Those full lips had been petal-soft and she'd tasted of chocolate… I'd always had a weakness for chocolate.

I didn't want to wake her. She looked so peaceful curled up in the seat, her hands tucked beneath her cheek like a child. Her long silky lashes fanned out over her cheekbones and didn't even twitch. The trip to Madrid and then back to England again must have exhausted her. She hadn't been well back in Madrid either, though she'd regained some colour, which was good.

A good thing, too, that she didn't know how much it had cost me to keep my distance from her the second I saw her, not to sweep her up into my arms and carry her away, make her mine the way the beast inside me wanted to.

And she would never know.

Distance was the only way to keep her safe, and detachment the only way to control my own urges, so distant and detached I had to remain.

However, if I was going to transfer her to the helicopter that would take us to Glen Creag, the only way I could do so was to carry her. It was a physical distance I didn't want to close since I couldn't trust myself—not after that night in the garden—but I didn't want anyone to touch her either. So I braced myself against the desire she always generated in me and gathered her up in my arms.

She'd no doubt be very unhappy with me taking her to Scotland instead of London, and she'd probably have words to say, but I didn't want an argument now. She needed her sleep, and I was concerned by how sick she'd been in Madrid. I'd get a doctor to look over her in the morning, but until then she would sleep safe in my arms.

You want her there. You want to keep her there.

Reflexively, I forced the thought away. Regardless

of whether I did or not, the need was dangerous and I couldn't allow it.

I bent and gathered her up gently. She was very soft, and very warm, and when I straightened she made a small sound, curling into me and pressing her cheek against my shoulder.

She trusts you.

There was a hot, tight feeling behind my breastbone, and for a second I found breathing difficult. I wanted to gather her closer and guard her against every bad thing.

But that bad thing was me, which made it difficult—especially when I'd already made one catastrophic mistake with her already.

I would need to be doubly on my guard now.

The leftover anger from earlier in the evening knotted in my gut. Anger at myself and my inability to control my emotions, even after all these years and all the painful lessons my father had taught me. Anger at the mistake I'd made three months earlier that had led to both of us being in this position.

And, unfairly, anger at her for being who she was—the one bright spark in my life. All smiles and joy and a sharp, vital beauty that cut at my soul and tempted me beyond reason. She'd given me her trust and allowed herself to be vulnerable. That way lay only pain as I had good reason to know.

Ignoring the emotion, I carried her out of the jet and down the stairs to the Tarmac. A helicopter, our final mode of transport for the night, waited not far away, the rotors already spinning.

The sound didn't seem to disturb her. She simply

snuggled into my shoulder, turning her face against the wool of my suit jacket as if the runway lights bothered her.

I tightened my grip.

Some of my staff came to assist me into the helicopter, but I refused them. I didn't want anyone else touching her and nor did I want to release her. It was a possessive urge from my baser self that I tried never to allow, but it was late, and it had already been a hectic night, so I indulged it.

He can't see you any more. He's dead.

The thought came out of nowhere, but I ignored that too.

Protecting her—protecting everyone—from my father had become second nature, and apparently it didn't matter that the bastard was now gone. The reflex was still there.

Eventually we were settled comfortably in the helicopter. I didn't bother putting a headset on Jenny. If the noise of the machine hadn't woken her already then nothing would, and putting a headset on her wouldn't make her lying in my arms very comfortable. I didn't want anything to disturb that. It wouldn't be a long flight anyway.

The helicopter lifted off and soon we were flying into the darkness of the Scottish Highlands.

I allowed myself a moment to relax, automatically shifting the soft weight of the woman in my arms so she would be more comfortable. The movement made me acutely physically aware of her. The press of her rounded breasts against my chest. The curve of her rear settling against my groin.

Soft. Hot.

She smelled of something fragile and sweet, like magnolia blooms or rose petals, with an exciting, delicately musky scent beneath it. A scent that was all her and intrinsically feminine, appealing on a base level to the male in me.

Desire flared inside me, always so strong, and I found myself looking down at her, at the line of her cheek and the upturned tilt of her nose. She wasn't a typical beauty, not like her mother, but she had a warm, vital sensuality of her own that was even more attractive to me.

I'd assumed my marriage to Olivia would include sex, since children were part of the deal, but I hadn't felt any physical desire for her. We'd come together when we wanted to conceive, and perhaps for some release, but nothing more.

If she'd wanted to find passion elsewhere, I'd have had no problem with it, since she'd certainly never find it with me.

But... I couldn't do that with Jenny.

There would be no 'coming together' for the purpose of children, or even for release. My control had to be perfect, and she undermined it too much.

I should never have touched her at all, for example, let alone dragged her down into the grass and taken her like an animal the way I had three months ago. A moment of madness, that was what it had been. That and four years of holding her at arm's length, and the pressure of a constant hunger, a need I hadn't been able to get rid of.

A hunger I'd been fighting since the day I'd noticed that, at eighteen, she wasn't a little girl any more, but a soft, lush woman, with generous curves and the kind of eyes a man could fall into and lose himself gladly, the kind of mouth that could wreak havoc on his body.

And what made it worse was that it was a hunger that went deeper than merely curves and eyes and a soft, pouty mouth. Those I could find anywhere, with any woman. But her gentle warmth and kindness and empathy, the understanding that shone in her eyes whenever she looked at me, that smile… Those I could only find in one person: her.

It was shocking, that feeling. Appalling. Because Jenny was untouchable, pure. She was a bright light that had somehow never been dimmed by living in my father's house, and I couldn't be the one to extinguish it.

Distance was required, which meant our marriage would stay in name only. My self-control was equal to the task, I was sure. Sex was something I could easily do without.

What about her? What if she wants passion? Will you permit her to find it with someone else?

Somewhere deep inside, the beast roared in fury and denial, and I found myself holding her even more tightly, as if something or someone was trying to take her from me.

I gritted my teeth. This was why I had to be so very careful. I could *not* allow my possessiveness, my intense nature, to get free. It was an all-consuming thing if I didn't control it, and it would consume her if I let it.

But I wasn't going to let it.

Which would mean that my expectations of marriage would have to change.

Olivia and I had both decided that our lives would be more or less separate, even if we lived together. She had a company of her own, and while she'd needed my financial help to repay some of her late father's debts, I'd imagined that once the debts had been paid her main focus would lie with Wintergreen. As my main focus was Silver Inc. I'd envisaged us ostensibly living together, but that work and travel would mean we wouldn't spend much time together. And when we had children we'd no doubt parent separately.

However, Jenny didn't have a company. She worked in a shelter for the homeless. I had no idea about her living arrangements and whether they would be suitable for a child. There was also the question of her safety. Domingo had been a ruthless businessman and had earned himself many enemies.

I had tried to mitigate the damage he'd caused wherever I could, but I hadn't managed to prevent everything he'd done. Business deals he'd ruthlessly manipulated, companies he'd torn apart, people he'd fired…

There were people out there who hated me as much as they hated him, people who thought I was like him.

Aren't you, though? Didn't he tell you as much?

I ignored that thought completely.

I didn't care about people's opinions of me, but reputation was important, and the reputation of Silver Inc needed managing. I'd been planning to start improving that soon, but it would take time, and I didn't want Jenny to be adversely affected.

Jenny and our baby.

Something raw rippled through me at the thought of our child, another echo of that intense, possessive feeling. I ignored that too. Both of them would need to be protected, which meant I couldn't allow her to live separately from me.

I had to be there to protect her.

One lock of dark hair had fallen over her forehead and I reached up to push it back, then realised with a jolt that felt like a gut-punch that her eyes were open and she was looking up at me. In the darkness they looked black, gleaming from beneath her lashes.

'Where are we?' she asked huskily. 'What's happening?'

There was no fear in her voice, no anger either, and she made no move to get free. She sounded like a sleepy child on a long car journey.

'We're going home,' I said, conscious that a slight husk had crept into my own voice. 'Go back to sleep.'

'Home,' she murmured. 'That's nice.'

Then she closed her eyes, relaxing again into sleep, as if I was someone she trusted to hold her while she slept.

She shouldn't trust you.

I leaned back in the seat and lifted my gaze from her

face, staring straight ahead, out through the front windscreen of the helicopter and into the darkness.

No. She shouldn't.

No one should.

CHAPTER FIVE

Jenny

IT WAS THE sun streaming through the window and shining directly on my face that woke me.

I scowled and tried to burrow into the pillow, because I didn't want to wake up, but that sun was relentless. Plus, my stomach was starting to growl.

The night before had been a strange fever dream, full of the comforting roar of a jet engine, before it changed to the rhythmic sound of helicopter rotors. I had a confused memory of being carried in Constantine's strong arms across the Tarmac, and then feeling warm and safe as I lay against his broad chest, my stomach dropping away as we lifted off into the air. I'd no idea where he'd come from, since he hadn't been on the jet with me from Madrid, but for some reason I hadn't questioned it.

He'd murmured something about taking me home, and I hadn't ask why, if we were flying direct to London, we'd needed to be transferred to a helicopter. I'd been too tired to do more than accept it. When the helicopter had landed, I'd had an impression of wide-open spaces and a cold night wind, and then some stairs, and a long corridor that definitely wasn't in my little bedsit. But I'd assumed it was all part of the dream and had snuggled back down to sleep as soon as I was placed in a comfortable bed with a warm quilt drawn up over me.

I felt as if I'd slept very deeply after that, and it was strange that my alarm hadn't gone off. But I often woke up before it did, so maybe it wasn't so strange. As long as I hadn't missed work I'd be fine.

I yawned and opened my eyes, squinting through the beam of sunlight.

Then I blinked and sat straight up, my heart beating very fast.

I was not in my bedroom.

The room was huge—far bigger than my bedsit— with large windows currently hidden by long, heavy, pale linen curtains. The sun was coming through a gap, lighting the cream-coloured walls. Pale carpet covered the floor, and an antique dresser stood against one wall. There was a small table near one of the windows, a glass vase full of pale camellias sitting on top of it.

The bed I was lying in was huge and wooden, with a carved oak headboard, and it was piled with white pillows, a thick white duvet, and an expensive-looking, very beautiful patchwork quilt over the top.

A shock went through me.

It was clear that what had happened the night before had *not* been a dream.

Constantine *had* been there, and he *had* held me in his arms. We'd been in a helicopter, and he'd told me we were going home and to go back to sleep. But this was *not* home.

I swallowed, my mouth dry, my heart fluttering around in my chest.

Constantine had clearly been liberal with the truth, but no matter what he'd said to me that night in the garden, and no matter how angry I'd been with him, I trusted him. He'd never hurt me, so presumably wherever this was it wasn't anywhere terrible—there were camellias, for heaven's sake.

But…why?

I slipped out of bed, moving over to the windows and pulling back one of the curtains.

A view over a deep valley ringed by rocky mountains greeted me. There were forests at the foot of those mountains, and lying at the bottom of that valley was a pretty lake.

I shoved back the other curtain, my heart beating faster.

It appeared I was in an old stone manor house that faced the lake, with more stone buildings off to the left. The house was surrounded by green lawns that rolled into the tall, dark forests nearby and ended at the rocky shore of the lake.

The sun was shining on the lawns and the lake itself, turning the water a deep translucent green. On the foothills around the mountains purple heather bloomed, and the beauty of the little valley made me catch my breath.

No, it wasn't anywhere bad. And I was still wearing my cheap black dress, although someone had taken off my shoes and put me into bed. Had that been Con? Had he laid me in that comfortable bed? Pulled the quilt up around me?

And where was I? It looked a little like Scotland, though I'd never been there. But if it was Scotland, why was I here?

I turned from the view, smoothing my dress—a pointless task, since I'd slept in it and it was now hopelessly creased. A shower would be nice, but I had nothing to change into, and finding out what was going on was more of a priority.

Going over to the door, I tried the handle, half expecting it to be locked, and was surprised to find that it wasn't.

Outside was a long carpeted corridor with wood-panelled walls hung with landscapes and portraits. Windows at one end let the sunshine in, making it feel very light and airy.

It was very quiet.

Leaving the bedroom, I padded down the corridor in my bare feet until I came to a large, sweeping set of stairs that led downwards. The stairs were carpeted too, with more half-panelled walls, although this time the paintings on them were of a larger variety. A stag stood majestically before a green forest, his antlers glossy in the sunlight.

I went down the stairs and came to a large entrance hall. There were huge wooden double doors with glass panels to let the light in, as well as expensive silk rugs on the pale carpet. A few tables stood around, set with more flowers and a few sculptures, and—strangely for an entrance hall—there was also a big fireplace.

It was a gracious, luxurious space. A manor fit for an aristocrat.

Still not sure where to go, I went over to the first door I could see near the stairs and pushed it open.

Another large room opened out before me, a sitting room with windows on two sides, one giving a view of the rolling green lawns, the other looking out over the green water of the lake.

The room was full of light, its pale golden walls reflecting the sunshine and making the room seem warm and inviting. Comfortable couches upholstered in pale colours were scattered here and there, while a pair of worn leather armchairs faced each other near one of the windows.

It was a beautiful room, and I would have quite happily thrown myself down on one of the couches with a book, to settle in for a long morning of reading, if it hadn't been for the man standing in the middle of it.

He faced the door and his arms were folded, as if he'd been waiting a long time for me to walk through it.

Constantine.

My heart kicked hard against my ribs.

He wore one of his exquisite handmade suits, this one in dark blue-black wool and, standing there in the middle of the warm, inviting room, he seemed like a black hole, sucking away all the warmth and light, giving nothing back but ice.

His obsidian gaze swept me from head to foot, assessing me as if I was a machine that needed to be fixed or a problem he had to solve. Looking at the icy man standing before me, I thought it difficult to believe that the warm, strong arms holding me the night before had been his.

'I was wondering when you'd wake up.' His deep voice was detached, the lilt of his Spanish accent not making it seem warmer in any way.

I struggled to get my breathing under control and pull myself together, feeling like crying all of a sudden.

I'd thought I'd said goodbye to him in Spain. I'd thought I wouldn't have to see him again, or at least not for a long time.

I didn't want him to be standing there giving me the same coldly impersonal look he gave everyone else. As if that night in the garden had never happened. As if I was a stranger and not his friend. I didn't want him to be there at all.

I wanted to be over him—to give him that same look back, to feel nothing, the way he seemed to—and yet my heart ached and anger wound through me, and I couldn't decide whether to burst into tears or slap him across the face.

Neither was ideal. I'd wept humiliated tears in front of him once before, and I'd rather die than cry like that again. And as for slapping him, while that would be satisfying, like weeping it would also be humiliating. It would betray how badly he'd hurt me, and I didn't want to do that either.

I wanted him to think that I was over him, that I didn't care about him in any way. That his four years of silence didn't matter to me at all.

But it was difficult when he looked so immaculate in his suit, his short black hair glossy in the morning sunlight coming through the windows, that same sun outlining the perfect bone structure of his face.

His beauty had always made me catch my breath. And it wasn't something I'd only gradually come to see over the years. I'd always known it. Even as a child.

He seemed like an icy prince, noble and beautiful and stern, but lonely. Always lonely. Always working like a dog for Domingo, spending long hours in his office whenever he was home. I'd tried to get him to do things with me, like play card games or swim in the pool, or take me to the Prado Museum. But he wouldn't. He had no time, he'd said.

So instead I'd sat reading in his office, so he'd know that he wasn't alone. And I'd liked being near him. I'd liked the way he never told me to shut up when I talked, or that no one was interested in what I had to say. He'd never told me I had to be seen and not heard, because if I wasn't no one would want me for a stepdaughter and then Mummy and I would go hungry.

I'd liked it that he'd listened to me, and I'd known he was listening because sometimes he'd responded. But I hadn't liked it when Domingo had come in and Constantine had sent me away. He'd never talked about Domingo, and whenever Domingo had been near him, he'd tense up, go as cold as ice. I hadn't been sure why, but even back then I'd known that whatever it was, the problem was Domingo, not Con.

He might have been my prince, but I had never been his princess. And I was still just Jenny, his short, round and plain stepsister. With no shoes on her feet and her hair in a mess. Wearing a cheap dress that she'd slept in and now was all creased.

Anger flickered through me. I'd never felt pathetic in front of him before but I did now, and I hated it. It was almost as if I wasn't good enough or didn't measure up. My mother was an expert at making me feel that way and I didn't need it from him.

I lifted my chin, about to say something cutting, when my stomach growled. Loudly.

Constantine's brows twitched. 'You're hungry,' he said coolly.

'The baby is.' I sniffed. 'I'm not.'

'Don't be ridiculous.' He said it without anger, his voice detached. 'We'll talk over breakfast.'

'No,' I said. 'We won't. I have nothing to say to you.'

He ignored me, striding to the door and going out into the corridor. I heard him issue a couple of orders and then he was back, one large hand catching me beneath the elbow as he urged me over to the armchairs near the window.

My anger flickered at his high-handedness, yet I was powerless to resist. His palm was warm against my bare skin, and it reminded me of the dream that hadn't been a dream, of his arms around me, my head resting against his chest, listening to the strong, steady beat of his heart.

I forced the memory away as he sat me down in one of the armchairs, then sat in the one that stood opposite himself.

'I've ordered breakfast.' His gaze pinned me like a black obsidian spike. 'It shouldn't be long.'

I sat rigidly in the chair, trying not to be aware of how comfortable it was and how my instinct was to curl up in it. A childish instinct, borne of trying my best to avoid my mother and her lectures on my appearance and my clothing choices and how I'd never get a man if I didn't make an effort, because I was already starting at a disadvantage due to my face. How I needed to smarten myself up, get some make-up, lose some weight, wear something more flattering. Because how was I going to get ahead in life if I didn't look the part?

Now, with Con sitting across from me, staring at me, I couldn't help but feel that same sense of judgment.

It's different, though. He's not your mother.

True. And he'd never once made disparaging comments about my appearance. In fact, in the months before I'd moved to London, a couple of times I'd sworn I'd seen heat there in his eyes.

But of course I'd been seeing things. And even if he'd opened his arms to me right there, right now, I wasn't going to fall helplessly into them the way I'd had three months ago. Been there, done that. My mother might be moved by a pretty face, but I wasn't.

I stared back at him, trying not to give in to the urge to lower my gaze under the pressure of his. 'Well,' I said, trying to sound as cool as he did, 'I think you owe me an explanation for why I'm not currently in my flat in London, don't you?'

If he noticed my tone, he gave no sign. 'I never promised to take you back to your flat.'

'The man who took me to the car told me I was going

back to England,' I pointed out. 'Which was the whole reason I went with him in the first place.'

'He wasn't lying. You were taken back to England.'

'But you—'

'But I what?' One black brow lifted. 'Scotland is part of the United Kingdom.'

So we were in Scotland. Good to know.

'But Scotland isn't England. And I didn't say you could take me to…this place.' I waved at the mountains and the loch outside.

'"This place" is one of my private residences. Glen Creag. It's in the Highlands.'

'That's great. But I don't recall mentioning an overwhelming urge to visit the Highlands someday soon.'

'You didn't. If you'd bothered to wait as I instructed, instead of leaving the mansion, you would know that we're here to discuss the question of marriage.'

An echo of the same shock I'd felt last night rippled through me. 'You said—'

'I said that I wanted to marry you,' he interrupted yet again. 'I meant it.'

'Why?' I was too taken aback to be angry this time. He couldn't be serious. He couldn't. 'You can't want to marry me, Con. You're engaged to Olivia.'

'Olivia is now out of the picture.' His gaze snapped to the door as a quiet tap announced the arrival of one of his staff, carrying a tray. 'Over here, if you please.'

A smiling, grandmotherly older woman came over and set the silver tray down on the little table positioned between Con and I. On it were eggs and toast, plus a bowl of porridge topped with cream and brown sugar.

There was butter and jam, a pot of tea, and a small white china espresso cup full of what smelled like the thickest and darkest of coffees.

'There you are,' the woman said in a thick Scottish brogue. 'Breakfast.' Then, somewhat shockingly, she laid a hand on one of Con's broad shoulders and gave it a gentle pat, as if he was a horse in need of soothing. 'Enough for you too,' she added. 'See that you eat. I won't have any of this "not hungry" nonsense.'

I stared at the woman in surprise, part of me tensing in anticipation of the cold, sweeping look of disdain that Con would no doubt direct at her.

Except he didn't.

'This looks excellent. Thank you, Mrs Mackenzie,' he said, scrupulously polite. Then he nodded at me. 'This is Jenny Grey. Jenny will be staying with us for a while. Please make sure that she is comfortable.'

Mrs Mackenzie gave me a big smile and patted him again. 'Don't you worry, laddie. I'll look after her.'

'N-nice to meet you,' I said, stammering slightly at the shock of Con being called 'laddie'.

'And you, lass.' Mrs Mackenzie gave a satisfied nod. 'Right. I'll leave you both to it.' Then she bustled out.

'Mrs Mackenzie is the housekeeper here,' Constantine said. 'If there is anything you need, tell her and she'll accommodate you.'

I nodded, distracted by the divine smell of the food and the coffee, and my stomach growled yet again, reminding me of how empty it was. No wonder, considering I'd emptied most of it on Con's shoes the night before.

Ugh. That was not a good memory.

Not that I should be remembering that, or even concentrating on the food, not when he'd just told me that Olivia was 'out of the picture'.

'You mentioned Olivia,' I said. 'What do you mean that she's "out of the picture"? How? And why?'

'The hows and whys are irrelevant,' he said. 'Eat your breakfast. I'll give you the details.'

CHAPTER SIX

Constantine

JENNY WAS GIVING me a mulish look, which was unlike her. Normally there was never any argument between the two of us. This stubbornness she was directing at me was new and I didn't like it.

I'd spent at least an hour downstairs, waiting for her to get up, and while I could have woken her myself, I'd wanted to make sure she had as much sleep as she needed.

Being patient was a strength of mine, and I hadn't thought waiting would be a hardship, yet I'd found myself pacing around and glancing towards the doorway, wanting her to be up so I could see her, talk to her.

I didn't want to admit that I'd missed her these past four years, but I had. Her lack was a constant ache deep in my heart, made worse by those moments in the grass three months ago. And now she was here I wanted to...

But no. Now she was here the question of a marriage between us needed to be sorted out as quickly as possible so that arrangements could be made. Then I could get back to dealing with the Valentin issue. I'd anticipated our discussion would be straightforward, because while she'd clearly have questions, she wouldn't refuse me.

I'd ensure she'd have the best medical care for herself and the baby, and obviously finances would not be a problem. She'd also be protected legally by taking my name, as would the child.

As to the practicalities, we would work something out. I was prepared to negotiate on our living arrangements. If she wanted to live in London I had no problems moving, since the Silvera mansion in Madrid wasn't a home to me. I'd been planning to leave it anyway, so we'd find a house together that would suit us both and the child. It wouldn't be a problem.

And apart from anything else, she loved me. That was what she'd told me that night in the garden, so surely marrying me would not be a bridge too far.

Except you can't love her back.

That thought tugged at me, but it was inconvenient, so I ignored it.

Jenny, however, didn't look as if she was desperate to marry me. Sitting opposite, her black dress creased beyond all hope of an iron, with her hair in snarls over her shoulders, she looked tired and dishevelled and extremely cross.

She also looked so beautiful she stopped my heart.

The memory of her in my arms, warm and soft and relaxed, rose to the surface, making me want to pull her back into them again. But I didn't move. Distance was crucial, otherwise this whole plan wouldn't work.

'I'll eat when I'm ready,' she said firmly. 'Tell me why you're not marrying Olivia and does she know?'

'I'm not marrying her because you're pregnant and she isn't. And, yes, she does know.' Technically, that wasn't correct, but seeing as how she was with Valentin I could safely assume she wouldn't want to marry me now anyway.

You should tell Jenny the truth. Tell her Valentin is back and that he took Olivia. Tell her that she's all you ever wanted, that marrying her would be your greatest joy.

But I couldn't tell her those things. Valentin's return was a separate issue that I didn't want to get into right now, and marrying Jenny wouldn't be my greatest joy. It would be my greatest torment. Because while she'd be my wife, she would never be mine. I couldn't allow it. The possessive part of my nature—the part of me that was my father through and through—would be too strong to deny and I couldn't expose her to that. I wouldn't.

'You don't have to marry me because I'm pregnant,' Jenny snapped. 'This isn't Victorian England, you know.'

I ignored her tone. 'One of the conditions for me marrying Olivia was that she would provide me with heirs.'

'I see.' Jenny's dark eyes were sharp. She looked like a small, round blackbird, eyeing me with disfavour. 'And if someone else happens to get pregnant? What then? Would you get rid of me as easily as you got rid of her?'

You are hurting her. You know how she feels about you.

And she would hate being anyone's second choice, especially given all the lies Catherine had drummed into her about herself. And they were lies. Catherine was a career gold-digger and, while I could understand what had driven her to it, I had never understood her desire to mould her daughter into her own image.

Jenny didn't have that hard, mercenary edge. She was softer, warmer. She trusted too easily and she gave her heart too readily. After all, she'd given it to me, the worst person in the world for her.

'No, of course not,' I said. 'No one else will get pregnant because I am not sleeping with anyone else.'

She blinked, her pretty mouth opening in surprise. 'So…what? You'll be sleeping with me?'

A thread of raw heat wound through me, making everything inside me tighten. *Dios*, I would love to sleep with her, her warm, lush little body pressed against mine. I could have her whenever and however I wanted her, sink inside her welcoming heat…

But I couldn't allow it.

'No. That is not the kind of marriage I'm offering you.'

'Then what kind of marriage are you offering me?'

'It will be one in name only.'

Her dark eyes went wide. 'What? Why?'

I steeled myself against her surprise. The beast in me wanted to tell her that I was mistaken, that it would be a full marriage in every way there was. But I couldn't.

Instead, I said, 'Because the purpose of sex would be to conceive, and you are already pregnant.'

'But I—'

'That is the kind of marriage I was going to have with Olivia, and I will not change it just for you.'

Disappointment crossed her lovely face, although she tried to hide it, and I could feel it tug at me too.

It was not what I wanted. Yet it was necessary.

'Eat your food,' I said curtly. 'You've had nothing since last night and you're looking extremely pale.'

The disappointment had ebbed from her dark brown eyes, but little sparks still gleamed there, signs of her stubborn spirit. A reminder that while Jenny Grey might look small and soft and vulnerable, she wasn't as defenceless as she seemed.

I still remembered the day my father had stormed into my study while she'd been curled up in her customary seat. I'd instantly known that he was in one of his cold, cruel moods and had tried to order her out of the room. When he'd been like that, anyone and anything had been a target, so I'd tried to make sure that the only target he found was me. I was as cold as he was, and I could take anything he threw at me.

Yet before I'd been able to speak Jenny had slipped off the chair and reached for my father's hand, taking it in hers and pulling on it. 'Mummy says you'll take me for a walk in the garden, Stepfather. Please? I love going for walks with you.'

I'd braced myself to leap over my desk, put myself between her and him, save her from whatever he was about to do. Yet before I'd been able to move, instead of raising his hand to strike her, or utter some casually cruel remark, he'd stared at her with distaste. Then he'd shaken off her hand and, without a word, turned and walked away.

She'd looked at me triumphantly and I'd realised then, with sudden insight, that she'd grabbed his hand on purpose. Somehow she'd known exactly what to do to make the terrifying Domingo Silvera uncomfortable enough to leave the room.

I'd never discovered what it was about Jenny that had stopped my father from being abusive towards her, but something had. And that was when I'd understood that if Jenny was in my office he wouldn't bother me. So I never told her to leave. And, while she'd just been a deterrent initially, I grew to like her soft, cheerful conversation and her laughter, filling up the cold silence of my study.

She had been a light to me even back then.

Now, she looked at me with exasperation and said, 'I'm your friend, Con, not a child you need to take care of. I'll eat my breakfast if I want to. And as for marrying you, the answer is no. I'm not and that's final.'

I stared at her, irritated. Her refusal was something I hadn't anticipated. I knew the idea of being looked after financially would remind her too much of her mother, but thought we could work out an arrangement where she earned her own money. And if sex was the issue…

Yes, what about sex?

The thought made me want to growl, so I shoved it away.

'Why not?' I tried not to let my irritation show.

'Because you don't love me.' Her voice was flat. 'You're only marrying me because I'm pregnant.'

'Of course I don't love you,' I lied—because I could never tell her the truth. 'We had that discussion three months ago. And what's wrong with marrying you because you're pregnant?'

The soft fullness of her mouth compressed. 'There's nothing wrong with it, but that's never been what I want, Con, and you know that. I want stability and security—especially after the kind of childhood I had with Mum—and that doesn't just mean money and a roof over my head. Those things are great, yes, but our child needs more than that.' Her chin rose a little higher. 'It needs to be loved. And so do I.'

The thread of anger pulled tight, making me tense. I didn't want to have this discussion. It was pointless when I could never give her the love she wanted. My love was too tainted, too toxic, and I would never wish that on her, never, ever.

Still, the possessiveness that had somehow woken up roaring, that wanted both her and the child, only tightened its hold.

What if I let her go and she married someone else? Someone who gave her what she wanted? Someone who would be a father to my child...

No.

The denial was so absolute there was no resisting it.

I could never trust another man with my child, or with Jenny. She saw the best in people. She never saw the worst. She might marry someone she thought was a good man, someone who could turn out to be even worse than I was, someone like Domingo...

Everything in me went cold. I would die before I allowed that to happen to any child of mine or to Jenny.

'Marrying me will give you both security and stability,' I said icily, putting all my will in my tone. 'They're a better guarantee than love.'

She gave me a strangely sympathetic look that I didn't understand. 'Are you sure about that?'

'Love is irrelevant to this conversation. You and I are friends, and that surely is enough. Do you really want to be a single mother? All on your own?'

'Are we friends, though?' Her gaze was very direct. 'When you haven't spoken to me for years?'

Guilt shifted inside me.

I couldn't tell her why I'd cut off contact with her, why I'd had to keep her at arm's length. I couldn't tell her that I longed to give her all the love she was craving, and all the passion too, but that that was a road I couldn't start down, no matter how badly I wanted to. Not when I knew how toxic my emotions could be.

So I ignored the question and said, 'I know you don't want to rely on anyone for money, but as my wife you'd never have to worry about finances again. We can come to some arrangement where you could have your own business and your own income. We can live in London, if you prefer. We don't have to stay in Madrid.'

'Con, I can't—'

'You can travel the world…buy anything you want.' I tried to think of other things that might convince her, other things she might want. 'Silver Inc already donates to and sponsors a great many charities, but more can always be given. The shelter you work at, for example. They must need money.'

She only stared at me. 'Have you finished?'

I could feel my jaw getting tight. 'Yes.'

'Good.' Her chin jutted with that stubbornness I was starting to dislike intensely. 'Because the answer is still no.'

My temper tugged at the leash I'd put on it. The beast in me was excited by the challenging signals she was sending, making bolts of heat arrow straight to my groin. I tried not to pay any attention, tried to concentrate on my detachment instead. 'What can I do to convince you? Anything at all, it's yours.'

'You can't buy my agreement, Con.' Her pretty features had softened and there was real regret amongst the sparks in her dark eyes. 'I'm sorry, but I have to be firm on this. I'm marrying for love, both for me and for my child, and that's final.'

Frustration coiled tight inside me, threatening all my emotional distance.

'So if someone else comes along,' I ground out, 'someone who says he loves you. You'll marry him?'

'If I fall in love with him too, then yes.'

'And what if you're wrong? What if he turns out to be a terrible person? What if he hurts you? What if he hurts our child? Because it's my child too, do not forget that.'

Her mouth softened. Was that pity in her eyes? 'I know,' she said quietly. 'Believe me, I've never forgotten that the baby is yours. But you don't have to worry. I will never fall in love with a man like that.'

Except she had, hadn't she? She'd fallen in love with me.

'Jenny,' I began, to say what, I didn't know.

But she only said, 'Con,' and put her hands on the edge of the table and gave me a very serious look. 'You need to take me back to London. We'll figure out something when it comes to the baby later, but right now I want to go home.'

'Jenny,' I began again. Because she had to listen to reason. I needed to explain myself further, more clearly.

'No,' she said calmly, regretfully. 'That's my final word.'

Then she pushed her chair back and got to her feet.

What? She was leaving?

My frustration intensified. Because she needed to understand. She *had* to. She was vulnerable, and so was our child, and I couldn't leave her unprotected. I had never done so before, and I wasn't about to start now.

'Sit down.' I tried to stay cold, yet that growl crept into my voice all the same. 'Sit down and eat your breakfast. I haven't finished speaking.'

Jenny merely shrugged before turning around and walking away.

I did not like that. I did not like that one bit.

'Jenny.' Her name came out low and harsh and I didn't bother moderating it. 'Sit down.'

But again she ignored me, going to the door.

'Jenny,' I growled.

She walked through it.

People did not walk away from me. People did not ignore me. People who knew what was good for them obeyed whenever I gave a command and they certainly never *shrugged*.

This concerned the safety of our child. *My* child. I wouldn't tolerate it.

I shoved my chair back before I even knew what I was doing and went striding after her. 'Don't you dare walk away from me. I haven't finished.'

But the corridor outside was empty.

I caught a glimpse of movement on the landing and started up the stairs after her, taking them two a time, gritting my teeth against the sudden and inexplicable anger that threatened to swamp me.

In the back of my mind a warning sounded. I was allowing my temper to get the better of me, that I needed to stay in control. But control had always been difficult with her. Heat and hunger consumed me whenever I was in her presence, and no matter how hard I tried I couldn't detach myself the way I normally did.

All I could think about was some other man hurting her, some other man hurting my child and me not knowing about it. Me not being able to stop it.

That had been my childhood—mine and Valentin's—and there had been no one to protect us, no one to save us.

I knew what happened to children at risk. I knew it intimately.

My anger pulsed like a giant heartbeat, and even though I tried to keep it contained I couldn't as I stormed down the corridor after her.

She reached her bedroom and disappeared into it, slamming the door behind her.

I stopped outside it, fighting to regain my control. 'Open the door. Open it now, Jenny.'

I did not like closed doors. Not at all.

'No!' she shouted from the other side. 'I'm not saying another word. I'm not marrying you, Con, and you can't make me.'

No? That was unacceptable.

She had to see reason. She *had* to.

I put my hand on the door handle and turned it.

Only to find that she'd locked the door.

A low growl formed in my throat and something dark exploded in my head.

A memory. Me, sitting outside Valentin's locked door, hearing nothing but silence from the room inside. Knowing how much he hated being confined. Knowing deep down that the reason he'd been locked in his room was because of me.

Locked doors. I *hated* locked doors.

My fury burst from the cage I'd kept it in, dark and unstoppable, propelled by the fear I could never escape.

'Get away from the door,' I ordered, my voice so low and guttural it didn't even sound like mine. And in the gap beneath the bottom of the door and the floor, I could see the shadow of her feet disappear as she did what I'd said.

Then I kicked it in.

CHAPTER SEVEN

Jenny

CON'S VOICE WAS barely recognisable, yet animal instinct had me stumbling back from the door before I could even think. Then it suddenly burst open, bouncing on its hinges and slamming into the wall with a crash, making me gasp aloud in fright.

He stood in the doorway, breathing fast and hard, and oddly, considering he'd kicked down my door, all my brief fear abruptly drained away.

There was nothing of the cold, detached man who had sat across from me downstairs, insisting that I marry him. Offering me all sorts of things except the one thing I wanted. The most important thing of all: love.

It had twisted my heart in my chest to realise that he didn't seem to understand why I'd want it. That he thought money and travel, him protecting me, would be enough. Then all that stuff about me falling in love with someone else…

As if I ever would.

As if he wasn't the only man for me and would always be.

He hadn't been listening, though, and that hurt too. Because he'd always listened. Now it was as if I was talking in a language he didn't speak and didn't want to understand.

I hadn't been able to bear it. So I'd got up and walked away.

Some part of me had been thrilled to hear him growling at me to stop, to sit down, that he hadn't finished speaking. Thrilled to hear his voice change, to hear all the ice melting and threads of anger lace through its darkness. I'd never liked confrontation, but there was something exciting about confronting him and making him mad. It meant that he cared about the things I said, even if the only hurt was to his pride.

Right now, though, it was clear from the expression on his face that this was about more than hurt pride.

His perfect features were hard with fury, his strong jaw set, black eyes full of flames. It was a glimpse of the burning, raging furnace of emotion that lay in the deepest part of him.

I'd seen that furnace only once before: in the garden that night.

My breath caught, the heat he radiated making something in me spark like dry tinder.

He strode towards me, and before I could move he'd grabbed my upper arms in his long, blunt fingers, his grip just on the right side of painful.

'Never lock a door to me again!' His eyes blazed.

He was so tall, so powerful. He'd just kicked in the

door and now he had me in his grip. He could crush me as easily as he'd crush a butterfly.

But I wasn't afraid of him. I'd *never* been afraid of him. His presence had been a cool balm to my own raw emotions, his study a place of peace. He'd never turned me away, never told me to be quiet. He'd never judged me or upbraided me for not being pretty enough, or intelligent enough, or good enough. He was a rock, a safe haven, a shelter.

He would never, ever hurt me.

And I loved this raw display of emotion. Because he never let himself go, not like this. Never, ever. The only time I'd seen him lose control had been that night in the garden. The night all the ice had melted, allowing the man he was beneath it to be set free.

A man who wasn't frozen all the way through, but who burned like the sun.

You did this to him. This was all you.

My heart was bursting with a complicated kind of excitement and a fear that he might do something I'd like, something that would make all the vows I'd made to myself about not falling into his arms go up in flames.

Yet as I looked up into his burning eyes I realised I wasn't the only one who was afraid. Underneath all that anger, he was afraid too.

Ignoring his grip, and the fury in his expression, I reached up and touched one of those perfect cheekbones, brushing it gently. 'Something's wrong,' I murmured. 'What is it?'

The look in his eyes flared, as if my reaction wasn't what he'd expected. Then his grip on me tightened, and before I could say anything else he bent his head and his mouth came down on mine.

I couldn't say that I hadn't anticipated it. And I couldn't say I hadn't longed for it with every cell of my being.

The kisses he'd given me that night I'd never forgotten, even if afterwards there had been nothing for me but humiliation. They'd been my first, hot and rough and intense. Feverish. As if all the heat inside him had been channelled into those kisses.

It was the same now.

He kissed me hard and with total ownership, his tongue pushing into my mouth, exploring me with a desperate intensity I couldn't fight. I shuddered, trembling as he let go of my upper arms and plunged his fingers into my hair, tugging my head back.

He tasted dark and hot, like strong coffee, and he ravaged my mouth like a pirate.

I shouldn't want this. I knew that deep in my heart. And allowing him to kiss me like this was a recipe for disaster. I should push him away, tell him no, say that he couldn't get around me that way.

But...he'd looked afraid. And the desperation I could taste in his kiss told me that something was wrong. He was hurting in some way and I wanted to soothe him the way I always had, ease his pain.

I didn't know what to do to help. All I could do was put my hands on his broad chest and lean into him, press myself against him. Let him know I was there and that he could take anything he wanted from me, anything at all.

For a moment that hot, dark, blinding kiss consumed my world. Then abruptly he tore himself away and turned, striding to the door and going out without a single word.

Leaving me standing in the middle of the room, trembling all over.

Instinct told me that going after him would be a mistake, that I needed to give him space to calm down, so I waited for my heartbeat to slow and the trembles to stop. My lips burned. I could still feel the pressure of his beautiful mouth on mine, still taste his heat. The imprint of his fingers on my upper arms lingered and I found myself rubbing where he'd gripped me, even though he hadn't caused me pain.

I had no idea what had happened. He'd been angry at my refusing his proposal, but something about me locking the door had set him off. And then, when I'd touched his face, I'd seen something else blaze. Then he'd kissed me hard and deep and desperate. Only to pull away the next second and leave the room without a word.

It didn't make any sense. Why had he kissed me? He'd told me that night, after he'd pulled away, leaving me lying on the warm grass, that it would never happen again. That it had been a mistake, an aberration.

But if it had, why had he kissed me again? There had been raw heat in that kiss and, yes, desperation. But was it for me? Or...had it been about something else?

Something else, it had to be. After all, he'd said that the marriage he wanted would be a platonic one. Not that I'd be marrying him anyway.

I swallowed and rubbed my arms again, ignoring how sensitive my mouth was, shoving the taste of him and the feel of his hot, hard body against mine from my head.

It was true. He could give me financial security, and stability too. A home that I wouldn't have to leave because Mum had been dumped by her latest man and we had to find a cheaper flat. And I wouldn't have to sleep with a chair wedged under the doorhandle, because her latest boyfriend was creepy and I didn't trust him.

Con could give me safety.

But it was also true what I'd told him downstairs, that security was about more than money, more than a nice house and a security detail.

My mother had spent years not only picking apart my appearance, but also telling me that I shouldn't be so sensitive, so emotional. That I needed to grow a spine and a hard shell because life was cruel, and you had to protect yourself from it any way you could.

I'd tried, because I'd loved my mother, and she'd been so bitter, and I'd only wanted to make her happy. She'd complained a lot about me being a barrier to her 'getting ahead', and even though when I was a kid I'd never known what 'getting ahead' meant, I'd known enough to realise that being a barrier was a bad thing. So I'd been obedient when she'd wanted me to be seen, and when she hadn't wanted that I hadn't been seen.

But that hadn't been enough for her. *I* hadn't been enough for her.

She'd gone from man to man, sugar daddy to sugar

daddy—for money, ostensibly, but I'd known money wasn't really what she'd wanted. She'd wanted love.

I didn't want my life to turn into hers—endlessly dragging my poor child around in a vain attempt to find it—and I knew that was what would happen if I married Con.

Only it would be worse. Because while I loved him, he didn't love me, and that would only turn into bitterness for us both in the end.

Though I shouldn't be angry at Mum. It wasn't her fault she was the way she was. She'd been young when she'd had me, and my father had dumped her as soon as he'd found out she was pregnant. She'd lived a hand-to-mouth existence after I was born, subsisting on a single mother's benefit until she'd found out that having no qualifications or work experience weren't barriers when it came to charming men.

Mine had been a lonely, uncertain, unsettled childhood, and I didn't want that for my child. So no matter how much a part of me wanted to give in, to tell Con that of course I'd marry him, I wasn't going to. I needed to be strong.

Eventually I went over to where my handbag rested, on a small armchair near the window, and extracted my phone. I assumed Con hadn't let my mother know what was happening, which meant that I needed to. Then again, maybe he had. He always planned for every eventuality after all.

I also needed to let the charity who operated the shelter for the homeless where I worked know what was happening, too. They struggled to get enough help as it was.

I pulled up the number from my contact list, only to realise there was no cell phone service. Well, great. So not only had Con brought me to his Scottish bolt-hole without asking me, I also couldn't tell anyone I was here.

Anger joined the tangled mess of emotion sitting in my gut, but before I'd had a chance to untangle it a soft knock came on the door frame. I looked up from my phone and saw Mrs Mackenzie standing in the doorway, bearing a silver tray carrying the breakfast I'd walked away from downstairs.

'Mr Silvera thought you might prefer to take breakfast in your room.' She had very blue eyes that twinkled as she smiled at me. 'Come on, pet,' she said, bustling in and putting the tray down on a small side table. 'Eat up, there's a good girl. Then you'll want a shower and some clean clothes, hmm? I'll find you something to wear.'

My mother's parents were both dead, so I'd never had a grandmother, and Mrs Mackenzie's grandmotherly air eased my lonely soul. So I didn't protest as she poured me out a cup of tea and arranged everything on the table, keeping up a stream of reassuring chatter.

The breakfast was delicious, and I felt better for it, and after Mrs Mackenzie had taken away the breakfast things I went into the huge en suite bathroom to investigate the shower. There was a deep clawfoot bath near one window, and a large tiled walk-in shower tucked away in an alcove. Everything was white and clean. I couldn't get my clothes off fast enough.

The water in the shower was hot and the pressure fantastic, and as I washed my hair and body I let myself think of nothing at all.

After I was clean, I wrapped myself in one of the large, white fluffy towels that hung on a rail, and went back into the bedroom.

The bed had been made and a dress laid out on the thick white quilt. It was a simple wrap dress in deep red, and as I bent to examine it I saw the fabric was silk.

Mum had always insisted that 'dressing the part' was important, so she was never without her make-up or her designer clothes—when she could afford them—and never less than immaculate.

'It's all about confidence,' my mother had told me. 'No one wants a limp dishrag.'

But I hadn't had any confidence. She hadn't been interested in my marks at school, and she hadn't wanted to hear it when I'd told her of my childhood dream to become a doctor.

'You don't need all of that,' she'd said dismissively. 'Get some work done on your face, stop eating pastries, and find yourself a rich man.'

That had been the day I'd realised that the women Con was constantly photographed with were always beautiful. They were always successful women too, models, fashion designers, politicians, CEOs. There had even been a world-renowned human rights lawyer, and I'd toyed with the idea of going to law school. But my marks hadn't ended up being good enough for medicine, let alone for law, and I hadn't been interested in fashion.

I didn't have the looks to be a model, or the contacts

to be a politician, or the ruthlessness needed to be a CEO. I couldn't be one of those women at all.

Ironically, it had been a conversation with Con that had decided me. I'd been complaining about how I didn't know what to do with my life, and he'd asked me what mattered to me most in the whole world. *You do*, I'd wanted to say, but I hadn't.

Beyond that, what I'd wanted was to help people. And, after more discussion, he'd helped me figure out that charity work was definitely within my skillset. Eventually I'd found a job at the shelter. That didn't depend on looks, or school marks, and no one cared what I wore. I was good with people, and I was organised, plus I'd discovered I had a talent for fundraising, which the charity was pleased about. And that had been enough.

Gingerly, I touched the fabric of the dress. It was warm and soft against my fingers. It had been set out for me, obviously, though I'd no idea where it had come from. Did Con have a selection of women's clothes here? Was it Olivia's, perhaps? If it was, there was no way it was going to fit me.

'Here we are, pet.' Mrs Mackenzie came bustling in again, this time with an armful of silky, lacy-looking garments. 'Some smalls for you.'

I blinked as she put what she was carrying down on the bed. Underwear, from the looks of things. 'But I—'

'Don't worry.' She smiled. 'Mr Silvera had some things bought for you in Madrid. They're all your size and will fit a treat. He says you're to make yourself at home, do some exploring of the manor and the grounds. If you need anything, there's a bell on the tray in the hall. Just give me a tinkle.' She gave me the same gentle pat on the shoulder that she'd given Con downstairs. 'And don't fret about Mr Silvera. His bark's worse than his bite.'

I wanted to tell that, yes, I knew that already, but she bustled off before I could.

I stared down at the lovely clothes set out on the bed and let out a breath. Well, I had two choices here. I could refuse the clothing and keep my cheap chain store dress. Call Mrs Mackenzie back and demand to be transported back to London.

Or…

I could put on the dress and find Con, demand that he tell me why he'd kicked down my door. Why he'd kissed me. Why, when he'd taken me so desperately three months earlier, a platonic marriage was all he was offering. Why, when he'd ghosted me for four years, he was so desperate to marry me now.

Ah, but it wasn't a choice at all in the end, was it? I knew what I was going to do already.

Slowly, I began to dress.

CHAPTER EIGHT

Constantine

I SAT IN the chair in the little crofter's cottage I'd had remodelled into an office, staring out of one of its windows. It gave a perfect view over the lawns and the soft grey stone of the manor house, with the dark green of the loch beyond it.

The crofter's cottage was ancient, with thick stone walls, and I preferred it to the panelled walls of the den in the manor house since it was very private and there was less chance of someone stumbling accidentally into it.

I allowed no one in here, not even the cleaning staff.

Since there was no service in the valley I'd had it fitted out with a satellite internet link, so I could work, and work was what I should have been doing.

I'd already put in a couple of hours, first making sure news of Valentin's arrival had been contained, before getting intelligence on what was happening in the Maldives.

Olivia was still being treated well, and was apparently in no hurry to leave. I wasn't worried about her. Valentin might have stolen her from me while also trying to take my company, but he was my twin. I knew him. And he'd loved her once. If what he felt for her now was even a tenth of what I felt for Jenny, then Olivia was in safe hands.

Valentin was probably expecting me to go after him, however. Which meant I wasn't going to, especially if Olivia was in no danger. She was a strong woman. That was part of the reason I'd chosen her as a potential wife. She could manage whatever nonsense he was engaging in. Their friendship as children had grown into something more as teenagers, and it had once made me jealous. At least until I'd discarded jealousy along with all the other emotions that used to trouble me.

At least until Jenny had come along.

I'd used to feel nothing at all when I'd thought about my brother, but there were reasons I'd never spoken to her about him, mainly because she would ask questions about him, about our childhood, about Domingo, and I'd known I couldn't tell her those things. Not when she'd had the uncanny ability to reach inside me and coax emotion out of me whether I'd wanted her to or not.

As if on cue, a small figure stepped out of one of the manor's doors and stood for a moment, gazing around, a brilliant splash of red against the grey stone walls.

Everything in me clenched tight. Valentin was abruptly forgotten.

Jenny. And she was wearing the dress I'd bought for her.

I gripped the arms of the chair, my fingers digging

into the expensive leather as the memory of what I'd done only that morning came flooding back. Of finding the door locked and something in my head exploding. Of kicking the door and watching it crash open. Jenny, white-faced, stumbling back.

I'd still been in the grip of that rage and I'd stormed in there before I'd even known what I was doing, grabbing her by her upper arms and roaring at her.

Her face had gone pale with shock, her dark eyes huge, and while a part of me had regretted scaring her, another had been savagely glad. Because now she would see why being in love with me was such a bad thing, why opposing me, pushing me, was dangerous. I would never hurt her physically, but I had no emotional control around her and I could hurt her in other ways. Ways I'd learned at my father's knee.

Except then she'd put her hand to my cheek in the gentlest of caresses. And she'd looked straight at me, past the anger, right down to the pain and fear I kept locked away inside. And she'd asked me what was wrong.

She'd always been able to do that. She'd always been able to see past my detachment, see the boy I'd once been years and years ago. The boy who'd rescued chicks from fallen nests and cried over dead kittens. The boy who'd once wanted to be a pirate or a cowboy, who'd loved his twin brother and had tried his best to protect him.

Jenny had reached out to that boy, and that boy wanted to reach out to her in return.

But I couldn't allow it. My anger and my stunning loss of control had been proof enough of that.

I shouldn't have kissed her, either. But I'd already been undone by the touch of her fingers on my cheek, and the depths of my own anger and fear had only undone me further.

Kissing her had been instinctive. The beast in me had been tired of distance and it had wanted her, it had needed her, and so it had taken what it could.

I'd expected her to protest or struggle, yet she'd melted against me the way she had that night in the garden, all soft and hot and giving. Making me want to take and take and take.

Dios. I'd thought my control around her was ironclad, that the distance I'd put between us these last couple of years had done its job. Yet every time I was in her vicinity that control failed, and nothing I did seemed to prevent it.

The figure in red moved away from the manor, following one of the white gravel paths that led down to the loch's pebbly beach. The wind whipped the dress around, flattening the red silk against her luscious curves. Even from here I could see them, full and rounded, inviting a man's hand.

I could feel myself hardening—a reminder of her physical effect on me—and every muscle in my body went tight.

I needed to do something about it because distance wasn't working. And that only left me with two options: either I gave that possessive part of me what it

wanted—which was her, in every way possible—or I
sent her away from me for good.

*But how can you allow that? When she's pregnant
with your child? What about if she falls in love with
someone else?*

That thought made me want to growl with fury and
denial, yet I couldn't force her to marry me if she didn't
want to. And the more she resisted, the more the beast
in me found it a challenge. It kept whispering that there
were ways to make her see reason, ways I *could* force
her, ways that my father used.

I could use her emotions against her, threaten to take
our baby from her when it was born if she didn't marry
me, for example.

Except that was the kind of tactic my father would
have employed, and my entire being rebelled at using
those kinds of tactics myself.

But if I sent her away I would never see her again.
And I would never see my child either. Because if she
fell for someone else… Well, I'd probably do something I'd regret, and neither of them needed to be exposed to that.

*Perhaps she'll fall for someone good. Someone
who'll treat her better than you will.*

That was true. That was a possibility and one I
couldn't deny her.

Still, I'd have to have them both protected in some
fashion.

I would never leave them with nothing.

A weight shifted in my chest at the thought—a
heavy, dull ache which I ignored.

The figure in red moved away from the loch, wandering over the rolling lawns surrounding the manor. Then she paused and I could see her turn her head, glancing in the direction of the crofter's cottage where I sat. Her curiosity must have been caught, because she started towards it.

I cursed under my breath. Clearly Mrs Mackenzie hadn't warned her not to come near the cottage, which meant I was going to have to warn her off myself. She couldn't be in here, not in my private domain. It was mine and I guarded it jealously.

Shoving back my chair, I crossed to the door, pulling it open and stepping outside.

She stopped dead as soon as she saw me, and didn't move as I went striding across the lawn towards her.

I found myself staring hungrily at the dress, pleased that, firstly, she was wearing it and secondly it fitted her deliciously. The wrap style suited her curves, highlighting her hourglass figure to perfection, while the red made her skin look creamy and struck warm tones from the deep chestnut of her hair. It flattered her eyes too, lightening the liquid brown into a beautiful copper.

As I came closer I saw her cheeks had gone pink, and she brushed a strand of dark hair behind her ear in a nervous gesture. Was she still remembering that kiss? Was it lingering in her memory the way it was in mine?

Fool. You cannot lose control again.

No, and if I couldn't even look at her without feeling as if I might, then the situation was even worse than I'd suspected. Sending her away was my only option.

My jaw ached, tension flooding through me as I

forced my attention from her pretty mouth, meeting her gaze instead.

'Oh,' she said breathlessly. 'I didn't know you were—'

'The cottage is out of bounds,' I interrupted. 'No one is permitted there.'

She glanced at the cottage, then back at me again. 'Okay, sorry. No one told me.'

'I'm telling you now.'

Her luscious mouth flattened, those intriguing sparks of temper glittering in her eyes again. 'You can be polite about it, Con. You don't have to bark orders at me like a drill sergeant.'

I was being an ass to her, and I knew it. Which wouldn't help matters.

'I apologise,' I said stiffly. 'I also apologise for scaring you before.'

She eyed me for a moment, as well she might, since apologising didn't come easily to me and I didn't do it very often. 'You didn't scare me,' she said. 'You never have.'

'Nevertheless. I should not have kicked the door in.'

Her chin lifted. 'And are you going to apologise for that kiss too?'

A flash of heat went through me. 'Do you want me to?'

Colour stained her cheeks and her gaze wavered, then flicked away.

I stared hungrily at her, noting the goosebumps rising on her arms. That slight breeze came directly off the mountains and was chilly. Perhaps we needed to be inside, where it was warmer, to have this discussion.

Taking a step forward, I caught her gently beneath the elbow. 'Come with me. We need to talk.'

She resisted. 'Do you really have to be so bossy?'

'Well, if you'd prefer to freeze to death then by all means let's continue this conversation out here.' I relented slightly. 'Please, Jenny. The wind is cold and your dress is thin.'

A complicated expression flickered over her face. 'Well…' she murmured after a moment. 'Okay, then.'

I should have let her go then, but I couldn't quite bring myself to do it. Her skin beneath my fingers was warm, and very soft, and I wanted to keep touching it. This might be the last time I ever got to touch her, so I kept my hand beneath her elbow as I urged her towards the manor.

'I'm sorry if I intruded,' she said again as I hurried her along. 'I thought it was okay to explore.'

'It is. I just don't want anyone going near the cottage.' I wasn't looking at her, my attention ahead, but I could feel her curious dark gaze on me.

But there was no point explaining—not when I was going to send her away—so I said nothing.

I thought she might ask why, but she didn't, remaining silent until we stepped through the front doors and into the entrance hall. Then I let her go, turning to face her.

Being outdoors had flushed her skin and made her dark eyes sparkle. She hadn't inherited any of Catherine's delicate blonde beauty, and neither had she any of Catherine's poise. Jenny was always fidgety, biting her lip and tugging at her clothes.

But she was beautiful to me all the same and standing in the hall, in the red dress I'd bought her, giving me a smile, she was even lovelier. Her skin reminded me of delicate pink roses washed by rain. Her chestnut hair lay in loose, glossy waves around her shoulders. There was a vitality to her, a sensuality I'd first noticed that day on the stairs, when she'd been waiting for me to come home.

She'd been all of eighteen, a woman grown, and my body had noticed even if my head had refused to acknowledge it.

All very good reasons to let her go now.

'So, what did you want to talk about?'

The flush to her skin had deepened. She'd noticed me looking at her. Which meant I needed to say my piece and get her out of my immediate vicinity.

'Speaking of that kiss,' I said. 'Yes, I apologise for that too. It should not have happened.'

This time there was no denying the emotion that flickered over her face. Disappointment. 'Do you really think that? Because I don't.'

I didn't want to hear that she'd liked it, that she still wanted me, even though I knew both things were true. I'd tasted the evidence in the heat of her kiss, in the way she'd melted against me, malleable as warm candle wax. I didn't want to feel the satisfaction that turned over inside me at the memory. It made me think of the garden, and the deep pleasure of her arms wrapping around my neck, of her body arching into mine, pressing all those sweet, soft curves against me. And it made me want to push her against the wall and take her now, ease inside her, keep her here in the manor house like the most precious treasure in my hoard.

She kept doing this. She kept undermining my control.

'I'm sending you back to London,' I said, ignoring her question. 'I'll arrange for transport to collect you in the morning, and you'll be home by tomorrow night.'

Jenny's lovely mouth dropped open, her eyes going wide. 'What? But before you were insisting that I marry you. In fact, you wouldn't take no for an answer.'

'I've changed my mind. I'm not going to force you into it if that's not what you want.'

I thought she'd be pleased, yet it wasn't pleasure or relief that rippled over her face, but shock. 'Why?'

'Isn't it obvious? You were very clear that you didn't want to marry me.'

'Yes, but...you were so insistent.' The pretty stain of pink had drained away, her cheeks now pale. 'Why did you change your mind?'

'As I said: you refused me, and I do not force women.' I searched her face. 'You should be pleased. You were clear that marriage isn't what you want.'

Abruptly, she looked away, smoothing down the red silk of her dress. 'It's not. I mean, one day. But...' Her smoothing hands paused, and she glanced back at me. 'What about the baby?'

'You and the baby will be taken care of. We can arrange the details later.'

'Details?' she echoed faintly, as if the word held no meaning for her. 'Right.'

I frowned, trying to follow the expressions on her face, because she wasn't acting at all the way I'd expected her to. 'This is what you want,' I said again. 'Isn't it?'

'Oh, yes, it is.' Her smile had returned, but it looked forced. 'Yes, absolutely.'

Yet from her expression it appeared to be the opposite. Curiosity tightened inside me. Why wasn't she pleased? She didn't want to marry me—not when I couldn't give her what she wanted—so why was she disappointed?

But I couldn't start thinking like that. I had to cut her out of my life and that started now.

'Good.' I made my voice cold and hard. 'Once you're back in London we will not see each other again.'

Her forced smile faded. 'What do you mean?'

'I mean, apart from being the mother of my child you will no longer be a part of my life.'

She searched my face as if she didn't believe me. 'You're serious?'

There was a dull ache behind my ribs, growing stronger, becoming pain. I knew this wouldn't be easy—not for her or for me—yet there was no other option.

There was too much of my father in me.

'I wasn't myself this morning, and I cannot risk you being harmed or scared by my behaviour. I'm not an easy man to be around, Jenny, so it's better for your sake if you are not.'

She was still pale. 'You *are* an easy man to be

around,' she insisted. 'I've been around you for years. I mean, not the past four years—which you haven't explained, by the way—but still… I don't understand. Is this an ultimatum? If I won't marry you, you won't see me any more?'

A thin thread of anger wound through me. As if I would stoop to using Domingo's tactics. Except he had couched his ultimatums with charm, so that the person he was giving them to wouldn't realise what he was doing until it was too late.

Domingo Silvera had been a charming psychopath, and no one had ever known his real nature except Valentin and I. We'd had to survive any way we could.

Valentin had survived by disobeying him at every turn.

I had survived by becoming him—at least on the outside.

Are you sure it's just on the outside?

Well, that question was why Jenny had to leave.

'I do not give ultimatums,' I said coldly. 'And I've already made the decision. You will be leaving for London tomorrow morning.'

Her face was white, her eyes very dark, and she opened her mouth to say something. But the pain inside me was too great.

I couldn't stand to be in her presence any longer, knowing that it would be the last time.

So I turned on my heel and went out.

CHAPTER NINE

Jenny

I COULDN'T SETTLE. It was a beautiful day, with the sun shining brightly in the dense blue sky above the valley, the loch reflecting back a perfect dark green. The purple heather on the hills around us was glorious and I contemplated going on a long ramble to explore. Yet I knew I wouldn't enjoy it. Not when all I could think about was what Con had said about sending me back to London. About me no longer being part of his life.

Mrs Mackenzie served me some lunch in a cheery dining room, which had a long, dark oak table and a huge fireplace at one end. It was pretty during the day, with the sunlight streaming in, but I could imagine it at night, with candles in the big brass candelabra flickering and a fire in the fireplace, all warm and cosy.

I'd had a lovely day exploring the manor and its grounds. It was such a beautiful place. And I should be pleased about returning to London. And yet…

Something cold sat inside me.

I'd had all those questions I'd wanted to ask Con,

and had faced him expecting a fight. Yet all he'd had to do was tell me he was going to send me home and my questions had gone straight out of my head.

I hadn't expected him to just…give me up.

He can't want you. Why would he?

I knew that was the truth, yet it hurt all the same. After that kiss I'd hoped… But, no, he didn't. It was only my stupid optimism. After all, he'd never given me any sign that he was attracted to me in particular, and that night in the garden, when he'd turned on me so ferociously, he'd been angry and upset. I'd thought afterwards that had been the reason he'd taken me. Not because he wanted *me* but because I was…what? Simply there?

Upstairs this morning, that kiss had been the same. He'd been angry and, again, I'd been there. It wasn't me he wanted, not *me*.

My gut twisted and my heart ached, but I ignored them.

I couldn't think about me. Our child was more important. And if Con was sending me home then that was a good thing, right? I would be the one to provide all the security and stability our child needed, and all the love too. Our child would grow up safe and secure and happy, the way I'd initially expected right from the start.

But shouldn't a child know its father?

Glumly, I moved a tomato around on my plate. I wanted to tell myself that of course a child didn't absolutely need to know its father. I'd never known mine and I was fine, wasn't I?

Then again, perhaps if my father hadn't left my

mother I'd have had a more stable upbringing. Perhaps if he'd stayed for my birth he might have wanted me. I might have gone to live with him, and things might have been different…

Except that hadn't happened, and things weren't different.

And by refusing marriage to Con you're denying your child the chance to know him and for him to know his child.

My fork dropped onto my plate with a clatter and I stared down at it, unseeing.

I couldn't deny him that. It wasn't right. Yes, it had been his decision to take himself out of my life and out of our child's, but there had to be a reason for it.

He hid it from most everyone, but he had a deep, caring nature that he'd never hidden from me. Once, back when I was eleven, I'd found a tiny nest of sparrow chicks that had fallen out of a tree in the mansion's garden. The mother bird had been nowhere to be found, so I'd picked the nest up and taken it straight to Con.

I'd known he would help and he had. He'd taken that nest to his study, kept the heat cranked up so the chicks would be warm, and then we'd both sat down at his computer to look up what to feed them. The nest had stayed in his study for a couple of days, and we'd looked after those chicks together until he'd managed to find a local bird sanctuary. Then he'd transported them there himself.

He was a protector, a caregiver. And not just with birds. He'd always made sure that I had a blanket to snuggle under, and he'd made sure that my favourite drinks and snacks were always stocked in the mansion's kitchen. When I'd got older, we'd discussed his plans for Silver Inc, and how he'd wanted to improve conditions for employees. It hadn't seemed to be a simple thing, though I hadn't been sure why.

What I was sure of now, though, was that he'd be a wonderful father, and I couldn't deny him the opportunity to have that connection. Some part of me sensed that he even needed it. Which meant I couldn't allow my own conflicted feelings about him get in the way.

Yes, I wanted love. But my child was more important than my feelings. Con could give me everything I'd always hoped for except love, and while he might not love me, he would love our child. I was sure of it.

Then there was the issue of his donations. The shelter always needed money, and plenty of other charities did too. I could help a lot of people if I married him.

I picked up my fork and shoved the tomato around a bit more. I would be like my mother, of course, marrying a man for his money, and she'd be very pleased to know I was even contemplating it. She'd been encouraging me to get closer to Con for years. But, again, refusing him just because I didn't want to be like her was all about me. It wasn't thinking of our child.

I bit my lip, then speared the tomato with my fork and popped it into my mouth, chewing slowly as the determination that had driven me to Madrid to catch one last glimpse of him hardened inside me once again.

Marriage. It had to be marriage. But I wasn't going to let him have it all his own way. I had to demand a few things of my own, set some boundaries. Otherwise he'd think he could tell me what to do. I wasn't the little girl who'd curled up in his chair and had only wanted to please him. Who'd rushed to get him drinks or snacks, or talked to him when he was sad. The little girl who'd once thought he could walk on water.

No, I wasn't that little girl any longer. He'd seen to that.

If I had to give up what I wanted, then he'd have to give up what he wanted too.

The idea of a platonic marriage, for example.

He might not want me, but he'd had no problem pushing me down on the grass and taking me, just as he'd had no problems taking that kiss this morning.

And I wanted more. I didn't want a platonic marriage, not with him. And I suspected he didn't truly want one himself. Seriously, was he really expecting us to stay celibate for the rest of our lives? Did he think that one time had been enough for me, and as for himself he'd take his pleasure discreetly, with other women?

A burst of possessiveness swept through me and I very deliberately targeted another poor tomato, stabbing it viciously with my fork.

Absolutely not. That would not be happening. The molten core of passion at the heart of him was nobody else's but mine and I would have it.

He was *not* going to deny me.

Full of renewed determination, I got up from the table and helped Mrs Mackenzie clean up—even though she told me not to—then went in search of Con so I could inform him of my decision.

He wasn't around, however, which meant he must be

still in the crofter's cottage near the trees by the loch. He'd been very clear that the cottage was out of bounds, which was annoying.

Part of me wanted to go charging over there anyway, just to show him that he couldn't tell me what to do, but I decided that this time he could come to me, so I amused myself in the library that led off from the living area instead. It was a small but cosy room, with bookshelves lining every wall and a small window seat piled with cushions. Unable to resist, I grabbed a book and curled up with it, spending the afternoon reading as the sun warmed me.

I must have dozed, because the next thing I knew it was dark outside, and I was blinking up into Con's dark and disapproving gaze.

He stood beside the window seat, looking down at me, his arms crossed over his broad chest. His expression was as hard and cold as I'd ever seen it. He was virtually radiating ice.

'I've spent the past twenty minutes looking for you,' he said in frigid tones. 'Mrs Mackenzie is going to be serving dinner soon.'

I pushed myself up on the cushions, my heart thumping. I'd wanted to be ready and poised when I told him I'd changed my mind, not groggy from an unexpected nap.

He was already turning away from the window seat, clearly his duty to call me to dinner done, so I slipped off the seat and said, 'Wait. I need to talk to you.'

He paused and glanced back, his black gaze sweeping over me like a chill winter wind.

My red dress was creased, and my hair was a mess, so it came as a shock when that same cold black gaze lingered on my breasts, where the fabric had slipped, and then flicked lower, to where the silk had parted, revealing my thigh.

Instinctively, I went to adjust the fabric, then stopped. Because there wasn't ice in his eyes any more, but... heat.

My breath caught. The air between us was abruptly gathering weight, becoming dense and shot through with electricity.

A muscle ticked in the side of his strong jaw, his eyes gleaming with a dark fire.

Did he...want me? Was that what I was seeing in his eyes? He wasn't upset or angry, and yet...

A wild, intoxicating heat swept through me as I realised that, yes, it was definitely fire in his eyes, and it was directed at me. Short, plain, dumpy Jenny. Then hard on the heels of that realisation came another: I'd assumed I had no power when it came to him, that all the power was on his side. I'd always wanted him, but he didn't want me, and that was the end of it. He was beautiful, powerful and rich, while I was none of those things.

But that wasn't quite true, was it?

My mouth went dry, my heart rate through the roof. I'd thought I'd have to work at convincing him to give me a full marriage, but maybe I wouldn't.

Maybe I had some effect on him after all.

To check, I bent to adjust the silk around my thigh, while at the same time allowing the fabric around my breasts to gape. When I glanced up at him from beneath my lashes, trying to be covert about it, I noted where he was looking. And it wasn't at my face.

A thrill went through me, electric and hot.

It was me, wasn't it? I did affect him.

Do you, though? Or is it just your breasts? Your mother always did say that men are easily distracted by a low-cut dress.

I shoved that thought away. It didn't matter whether it was me or not; what mattered was the small amount of power my femininity afforded me. And while it felt wrong to use it, since it was the kind of power my mother had always thought so important, it was still power. And I'd never had any before.

'What is it, Jenny?' he asked, his voice not quite as cold as it had been a second ago.

Slowly I adjusted the silk at my breasts, not missing how his gaze followed the movement of my hands. 'I've been thinking,' I said breathlessly, 'about your marriage proposal and about leaving, and I think I might have been a bit…premature.'

Constantine went very still, and this time his gaze met mine with the force of a hammer-blow. 'What did you say?' His voice was quiet and icy and deadly.

I lifted my chin, looked him straight in the eye. 'I said, I've changed my mind. I don't want to go back to London. I think I'll accept your proposal and marry you instead.'

CHAPTER TEN

Constantine

JENNY STOOD WITH the window at her back, the red silk dress now firmly wrapped around her curves, her hair in a loose dark skein hanging down over one shoulder.

I should have been paying attention to what she'd said, because it was important. But I couldn't get the sight of all that pale, creamy skin she'd flashed as she'd adjusted her dress out of my head. Or the glimpse of the red lace bra she was wearing underneath it.

The night we'd had sex, I hadn't seen her naked. She'd been in a dress that hadn't suited her, and all I'd wanted to do was strip her bare, see her glory for myself. Except that night there hadn't been time.

There was time now, though, and I could see myself tugging the tie at her waist and pulling away the red silk. Noting how the red lace of her bra cupped her pretty breasts, then putting my hands on them, stroking her satiny curves, tasting her. I'd lift her onto the window seat and rip away her underwear entirely, so she was naked, and then I'd—

'You did hear me, didn't you, Con?'

I blinked, ruthlessly grabbing my thoughts from the gutter and directing my attention back to her. Because, yes, what she'd said was important. Vitally so.

'You've changed your mind,' I said. 'You want to marry me after all, correct?'

Her cheeks were flushed, as if she'd read my mind and seen all the dirty things I wanted to do to her, and her warm brown eyes darkened.

'Yes,' she said. 'I've been thinking about it. It's not right for our child not to know you. I never knew my father, and maybe if he'd stayed things might have been different. But he didn't, and I… I don't want that for our baby.'

Heat flashed through me, an electric current that seemed to charge every part of me. My heartbeat was fast, my body hardening, that possessive, animal part of me already howling in triumph.

I wanted her. I wanted my baby. I wanted a family. I wanted *everything*.

But you can't. You're going to send her away because that's your best option.

Yes, that *had* been the best option when she'd refused me. She wasn't refusing me now.

I didn't move, keeping myself very, very still. 'I have said I will provide for you. Marriage isn't a requirement.'

'I understand that.' Her delicate hands fluttered. 'But it's not just about our child needing its father. I think you might…need your child, too.'

Every muscle in my body ached with tension, with

longing, because she wasn't wrong. I had no idea what kind of father I'd be, but I knew exactly what kind of father I *wouldn't* be. And whether I needed a child or not was beside the point.

I would have one.

A child that was mine to protect. Mine to keep safe.

I could not give that up.

'Very well,' I managed, forcing the words past the urge to growl that rose up inside me. 'But I still won't ever be able to give you love. That hasn't changed, Jenny.'

'I know.' Her fluttering hands stilled. 'But that brings me to another point. I don't see why you get to have it all your way. If I have to give up something, then you have to give up something too.'

My patience was thinning, my blood running too hot for me to be near her. 'And what should I give up?' I demanded gracelessly, needing to be away from her.

Her dark gaze was direct. 'A platonic marriage.'

I froze, every muscle, every cell in my body, electrified. 'What?' My voice sounded hoarse, unlike mine.

The colour in her cheeks deepened. 'I don't want to be celibate for the rest of my life, and I don't want another man. I don't want you going elsewhere for s-sex either.'

The beast shifted inside me, acquisitive, possessive. The hunger of a boy who'd been denied everything precious to him. The desperation of a man who now realised there had only been one thing he'd ever truly wanted.

Her.

As a child, I'd been forbidden any emotional attachments, and as an adult I still had to be careful. Because my father had had no compunction in using emotional attachments to get what he wanted. He hadn't cared who he hurt in the process, but I had, so I'd made sure that no one got close to me. I'd kept my distance by being hard, by being ruthless, by being cold.

But Jenny had somehow got past all my defences and found her way into my heart.

I still remembered the day I'd fallen in love with her. I'd returned to Madrid after an extremely hard six-month stint in the States, setting up a new Silver Inc company office.

I'd come home very late and headed straight to my room, only to find Jenny sitting at the top of the stairs dressed in nothing but an oversized T-shirt. The moment she'd seen me she'd leapt to her feet and her face had lit up as if someone had turned a light on inside her.

It had been me she was waiting for. Me who'd turned on that light.

'I just wanted to tell you that I'm so glad you're home,' she'd said. 'And that I missed you.'

People were afraid of me. They never lit up when I walked into a room. They were never glad I was home, and they certainly didn't miss me.

How could I not have fallen in love with her in that moment? How could I have resisted?

And I hadn't resisted. But I'd known that there could be nothing at all between us. She'd been only eighteen and I nearly ten years older. My emotions had been intense, toxic things that I would never expose her to.

So I'd distanced myself from her. I'd pushed her away.

That had hurt her, I knew that, and I knew if I denied her now I would hurt her again.

I didn't want to do that. I didn't want to hurt her, not any more. And my own denial wasn't working.

We didn't *have* to have a platonic marriage. Not if I was careful. I was a master at cutting my emotions off, and maybe allowing myself a physical relationship with her would even help matters. It might be a safety valve.

I could still keep her safe. I could.

'Are you sure that's what you want?' My voice had deepened, got rough, and I let it. 'A physical marriage?'

She was blushing furiously. 'Yes.'

'You must be sure,' I said roughly. 'You must be very, *very* sure.'

Some of my desperation must have shown in my voice, because she gave me a worried look. 'Yes, of course I'm sure. Why?'

I couldn't keep still any longer. If she wanted to know why then I would show her.

I stepped forward, crowding her against the window seat, luxuriating in the sexual tension that pulled taut between us. She gave a little gasp, her dark eyes widening. Then I leaned forward, putting my hands on the cushions either side of her, caging her with my body.

'This is why,' I said, and gave her a glimpse of the beast that lived in my heart, the one that wanted her with a desperation that bordered on madness.

I heard her breath catch, saw her pupils dilate. A hectic flush bloomed over her cheeks, the pulse at the base of her throat accelerated.

Disappointment was already gathering inside me because I knew that one glimpse would be enough. She'd change her mind. I would frighten her and she wouldn't want any part of me, not again.

She smelled delicious, fresh and sweet. Pushing myself away from her would be difficult. But I would do it. I'd already frightened her twice since we'd arrived here.

There wouldn't be a third time.

'If you're trying to scare me,' she said huskily, 'you're doing a terrible job.'

My whole body went taut. 'Jenny—'

'I'm not afraid of you. When will you believe me?'

The chains on my control began to loosen and I leaned forward even more, unable to help myself. I inhaled her scent, my breath against the soft, tender skin of her cheek. 'Sex is all I have to give you.' I tried not to growl. 'There won't be anything more than that. Not ever. Do you understand?'

'Yes.' Her voice was patient, as if she was trying to soothe me. 'I understand.'

But I didn't want to be soothed. I wanted to let go of my control, my restraint, let go of everything and take what was mine.

I angled my head, brushing my mouth along her jaw, intoxicated by the scent of feminine arousal and her own intrinsic sweetness.

'Tell me to stop and I will,' I murmured, easing forward, my body almost pressing against hers, a delicious agony. 'I will not hurt you. I will never hurt you.'

'I know you won't.' She took a ragged breath. 'Ask me, Con. Ask me, please.'

I could hear the note of desperation in her voice. It was the same desperation that lived in my own heart, and even though the logical part of me was telling me this was a mistake, I couldn't refuse.

'Marry me, Jenny,' I said. 'Be my wife.'

She gave a husky laugh. 'It's supposed to be a question, not an order.' But she must have seen that I was beyond amusement at this point, because her smile faded. 'Yes. Yes, I will be your wife, Constantine.'

A deep satisfaction swept through me. All the tension in my muscles faded, the beast inside me quietening. As if now she'd agreed to be mine it was content.

The man, however, was not. The man was starving.

I leaned in again, putting my mouth near her ear. 'Stay still,' I said. 'Stay very, very still.'

She did as she was told and I inhaled again, breathing in her scent, indulging myself utterly. I was hard, and I didn't resist, letting desire tighten its grip.

'You're mine now.' I bent to nuzzle against the side of her neck, brushing my mouth over her skin. 'Every part of you is mine.'

She was shaking, but she didn't move.

My satisfaction deepened, a sharp, intense pleasure I'd never allowed myself. It was addictive to have this, to indulge myself so completely, and perhaps it was a mistake. But, no, I could have her and keep my emotions separate. That was what I'd spent my life doing, after all.

I nuzzled into her throat, enjoying how she trembled, then put my mouth over her leaping pulse, the sweet, salty flavour of her skin on my tongue.

A breathy sound escaped her, honing my desire.

I sucked gently, tasting her frantic heartbeat. There would be a mark there in the morning and the thought pleased me.

I lifted my head and glanced down into her face. Her dark eyes were black and glittering as they met mine. I lifted one hand from the cushions and took hold of the tie of her dress, tugging on it.

She shivered, but made no move to grab the fabric as it fell away from her body, the red silk slipping open to reveal her.

My breath caught.

She was so very, very perfect. Even more so than I'd anticipated. Full breasts and rounded hips and thighs. She wore the red lace underwear I'd bought for her, the gaps in the fabric giving me a glimpse of soft pink nipples and the dark curls between her thighs.

Now she moved, lifting her hands as if to cover herself, but I grabbed her wrists before she could and held them down at her sides.

'No,' I ordered roughly, unable to tear my gaze from her beautiful body. 'I want to look at you.'

Another shiver went through her, but she didn't try to pull away. Her breathing was short and fast and ragged, and that red flush was creeping down her neck and over her chest.

'Beautiful.' I let my gaze sweep slowly over her creamy silky skin, her full breasts, her elegant, narrow waist, her curvaceous hips and thighs.

Her lashes fell, veiling her gaze, and I wasn't sure

why. But then I had an inkling. It was Catherine and all the lies she'd told Jenny about herself.

It made me furious to think how she wasn't valued by the one person who should value her, but it wasn't the right time to talk about it. I was impatient, and hungry, and I could think of better ways to let Jenny know how beautiful she was.

I let go of one of her slender wrists and put my fingers against her throat, stroking over her frantically beating pulse and the red mark I'd left on her skin there.

'You are exactly what I want,' I said fiercely. 'Exactly.'

She felt so soft, and she made another little sound as I let my fingers trail down over her chest, brushing lightly over the curve of her breast and then down further, following the line of her hip to her rounded stomach.

I stroked the little bump where our baby lay, allowing the fierce possessiveness to grip me, and then I let my fingers move over it and down further.

'C-Con...' she whispered as my fingers grazed over the lace between her thighs. It was damp, the evidence of her arousal slick against my fingertips.

Hunger wound its way around my soul, tightening until I could hardly breathe.

I dropped to my knees in front of her, pushing her back against the window seat, then tore apart the thin silk that was in my way.

She gasped as I touched her, stroking the soft, sensitive folds between her thighs, feeling soft curls and moisture and heat, and then she gasped again as I leaned forward, pressing my mouth to her stomach, trailing kisses down over it until I reached the salty heat of her.

'Oh… Con…' Her voice was ragged, a tremble shaking her.

When I licked my way inside her she jerked against me and cried out.

She tasted delicious, a delicate feast I couldn't get enough of, so I hooked her thighs over my shoulders, gripping her hips as I tasted her, deeper and more fully.

She fell back onto the cushions, crying out yet again as I pushed my tongue deep inside her.

She was mine now, every part of her, and I was going to take my own sweet time exploring her.

Her fingers curled in my hair, gripping me tight, and she shook beneath my hands. But I didn't rush. I feasted on her, making her cry out and sob.

And only when I was ready did I give her what she was begging for, making her sob my name as the orgasm came for her.

CHAPTER ELEVEN

Jenny

I LAY GASPING against the window seat cushions, pleasure still cascading through me. I couldn't move, could only stare at the ceiling, feeling as if I'd been shattered into a million tiny, glittering pieces.

Con had broken me, and I wasn't sure I wanted to be put back together again. Or maybe I did, if only so he could break me again like he had just now.

I'd told him I didn't want a platonic marriage and I'd thought I understood what that meant. Except I hadn't. Not really.

Oh, I'd seen the flare of black fire in his eyes as I'd told him I'd changed my mind, that I'd marry him after all. And I'd sensed the tension in the air growing tighter, hotter, as I'd said he'd have to give up the idea of a sexless marriage.

He'd asked me if I was sure, and I didn't know why he'd bothered to ask.

So he'd shown me.

It was as if I'd poured petrol on a smouldering fire.

Flames leapt in his eyes and he'd come closer, pressing me back against the window seat, letting me know that it wasn't just a fire that burned inside him, it was a volcano.

Perhaps he'd thought his passion would scare me, but that had been impossible, because all I'd wanted in that moment was him.

I'd ignored what he'd said about love. All I'd been able to focus on was the heat in his gaze, and when he'd whispered that every part of me was his my soul had shivered.

I'd felt self-conscious as he'd pulled away my dress, because he'd never seen me naked and I wasn't anything like the other women he'd been with. I wasn't tall, willowy Olivia, for example.

Except then he'd told me that I was exactly what he wanted, and then he'd touched me so softly, delicately, making me feel precious. He'd kissed me. He'd dropped to his knees before me. He'd…tasted me, making it very obvious that he was enjoying every second…

It had been the most erotic thing I'd ever experienced.

I shut my eyes, conscious that I was wearing only a bra and he was still kneeling on the floor, my thighs over his shoulders, my most secret places laid bare for him to see.

I tried to move, but he laid a firm hand on my stomach, pinning me. 'Don't,' he said, his voice rough with desire. 'Open your eyes, Jenny. I haven't finished.'

Unable to resist the command, I opened them in time

to see him rising from his position on the floor, his eyes blazing.

There was nothing left of his cold armour, nothing left of the glacier. He was burning with a raw heat that ignited me, burning my self-consciousness abruptly to the ground.

I had done that to him. While he might have broken me, and left me shattered, I had also broken him. I—short, plain, Jenny Grey—had broken the most powerful and feared man in Europe.

I pushed myself up, not bothering to cover myself. I didn't look away. I met his gaze and held it.

He didn't look away either, his hands dropping to his belt. He didn't rush. He took his time undoing it.

My mouth was dry, desire gathering inside me despite the shattering orgasm he'd already given me not moments ago.

This is a mistake. You know this will never be enough for you.

Maybe. But it was too late now. He'd asked me to be his wife and I'd accepted. And no power on earth would make me take it back.

'I want you, Jenny. Right here. Right now.'

Ferocious intensity burned in his eyes and I knew it was for me. *Because* of me. And that gave me power, a confidence I hadn't known was inside me until now.

'Yes,' I said thickly. 'Yes, please.'

His hands dropped away, his belt undone. I leaned forward, my fingers shaking as I undid the button on his trousers and unzipped his fly. I could feel the pressure of his gaze on me. He was watching me so avidly it was amazing I didn't combust on the spot.

'Your hands are shaking.' His voice was deep and laced with heat. 'Are you nervous?'

'No.' And it wasn't a lie. 'I just…want you.'

'Then take what you want.' His hands drifted to my hair, his fingers curling gently through it as if he relished the feel of it. 'I will be your husband and you can take from me as I take from you.'

Yet more confidence filled me, and I spread the fabric of his trousers, reaching to touch the long, hard ridge I could see beneath the fabric of his underwear. I felt him tense as I stroked him, my fingers trembling a little at being able to. That night in the garden everything had happened so quickly. It had been over before I'd known what was happening. But now I could touch him. Now I could see him.

I'd fantasised about him for so long, and now he was here the reality was…indescribable.

I drew him out. He was hot in my palm, and satin-smooth, and as I curled my fingers around him he made a harsh, very male sound. He reached down and pulled my hand away. The look on his face was drawn tight, his cheekbones etched, his jaw hard. He looked fierce, and hungry, like a wolf who'd gone without food for too long.

He didn't speak, pushing me gently but firmly back onto the cushions of the window seat. Then he slid his large, warm hands beneath my rear and lifted me, positioning himself. He pushed inside me in one smooth, hard movement, filling me completely, tearing a gasp of agonised pleasure from my throat.

He leaned forward, easing deeper, his gaze on mine as he placed his hands on the cushions on either side of my head. His black eyes were a furnace, burning me alive, while the pressure of him inside me made it hard to breathe. I'd forgotten how big he was, how the pressure and the exquisite stretch of my sex around his made everything sharper and more intense.

It was glorious. He was glorious.

He didn't speak, only looked fiercely down at me as he began to move, and I didn't look away. I couldn't. I was locked in his gaze, held there as surely as his body pinned me to the cushions.

He set a hard, relentless rhythm, sending fierce pleasure spiralling through my veins, and I reached up to grip his wrists, bracing myself against the shocks of his hot, hard body. He was still fully dressed, while I was only in a bra, and I found that so erotic. Especially as his gaze raked down my body, watching as I writhed beneath him, every movement he made coiling the pleasure tighter and tighter.

I could see he liked it, that it gave him pleasure to watch me, and that fed my pleasure too. I'd never had a man watch me the way he did, obviously liking what he saw. I'd never had anyone look at me with such possessive ferocity either.

He moved faster, harder, his teeth bared in a savage smile as he leaned down. 'Come for me, my Jenny,' he growled, before his mouth covered mine and his hand reached between my thighs to where we were joined, and he stroked me. Once. Twice.

I detonated, screaming his name against his mouth as the orgasm swept over me, turning me over and over and dragging me under.

Dimly I heard him make a harsh, guttural sound, felt his body slamming hard into mine, before he slumped on top of me, crushing me into the cushions.

He was heavy, but I didn't care. Once again he'd shattered me, all the pieces of me scattered on the winds and his weight the only thing holding those pieces together.

I didn't move, content to lie there under him, secure and safe beneath his heat.

Yet after a moment I wriggled under him and eventually he shifted, pushing himself up and away from me. I tried to sit, but he put a hand out, pinning me in place.

'No,' he ordered, his voice still husky. 'Stay there until I say.'

Puzzled, I did what he said, waiting as he adjusted his clothing and ran a hand through his short black hair. Then he bent, gathering my dress from the floor before pulling me off the window seat. He shook out the fabric and wrapped it around me with expert hands, tying the tie at my waist in a bow then smoothing down the silk.

He was so careful, so gentle, it made my heart ache.

Then he cast around for my underwear and picked them up. 'You can't wear these,' he said, examining the torn lace. 'I'll get you some new ones.'

Much to my shock, he folded them up and put them in his pocket.

I opened my mouth to ask him what he was going to

do with them, but he took my face between his palms and examined me carefully, and every word went clean out of my head.

His black brows were drawn down, his gaze sharp. 'Are you okay? Did I hurt you?'

'No,' I said. 'No, not at all.'

His gaze narrowed for a second, as if he didn't believe me, but then he nodded. 'You need to eat. You have a long night ahead of you.'

A thrill arrowed down my spine. 'I suppose that doesn't mean a night on the couch, watching TV?'

'No, of course not. After dinner I will be taking you to bed, where I can explore you properly.'

I shivered, anticipation collecting inside me. 'We don't have to have dinner. I don't mind if you want to go straight to bed now.'

His eyes gleamed, the banked flames leaping. 'Tempting. But food is important, especially when you're pregnant.'

I should have been thinking about what was going to happen next, about what exactly I'd insisted on when I'd changed my mind and told him I'd marry him. About weddings and living arrangements and all kinds of things...

But I didn't want to think about that. I couldn't even remember why it was important.

And when he took my hand, his fingers lacing through mine, I let him lead me to the dining room without thinking about anything at all.

CHAPTER TWELVE

Constantine

I NARROWED MY gaze at the computer screen, noting all my unread emails and deciding to respond to only two. One was to give a direction to my legal department to keep stonewalling Valentin's continued attempts to take over the company. The other was to remind my management team at Silver Inc that no mention of Valentin's return was to appear anywhere in the media, on pain of instant dismissal.

I didn't like being so autocratic with my staff, but I didn't want that leaked, not until the situation with Jenny had been well and truly handled.

It had been five days since she'd agreed to marry me and I'd kept her in bed, allowing my hunger free rein. I couldn't remember the last time I'd allowed myself such an indulgence, and it made me greedy. It made me want to cast all thoughts of wedding arrangements and the discussion of other practicalities aside so I could concentrate completely on her.

It was mid-morning already, for example, and I

could feel the persistent ache for her begin to build. I'd taken my time with her in bed this morning, hoping that would satisfy it, but it hadn't. The pull towards her, the demand for more of her presence, more of her time, just more of *her* was relentless.

So I'd taken myself off to the cottage to put some distance between us, thinking to immerse myself in work. But I couldn't concentrate. My head was too full of the satin feel of her skin and the silkiness of her hair draped across my chest. The tight clasp of her body around mine and the sounds she made when I was inside her.

I'd agreed to a full marriage thinking that I could master my emotions and that sex would be a good way to release the pressure. It wouldn't complicate matters. Except…that was turning out not to be the case.

Instead, sex had only opened up another avenue of fascination. I'd wanted to be careful with her because she'd seemed vulnerable, and I hadn't wanted to scare her. Yet I needn't have been concerned. She had a seam of pure steel that ran all the way through her, and a hunger that matched my own.

It was endlessly surprising to me that something so soft and unguarded should secretly be so strong. Perhaps, though, I shouldn't have been quite so surprised, considering how she'd had no hesitation in arguing with me since we'd got here. Whatever the case, I wanted to explore this hidden strength of hers in other, more interesting ways. Perhaps tonight I'd—

I growled, realising I'd been staring at my computer screen for a good ten minutes.

Unacceptable. I was supposed to *not* be thinking of her.

Shoving my chair back, I got up and turned to the line of bookshelves along one of the cottage's thick stone walls. Behind the books, hidden beneath a panel fashioned to look like a stone in the wall, there was a button. I flicked open the panel and pressed the button. A section of shelving slid to one side, revealing a door in the wall with a pad on it. I put my hand on it, my palm print unlocking the door.

The door opened and I stepped into the room beyond, hidden and protected from everyone but myself.

No one knew of this room's existence except the people who'd built it for me, and I'd paid them handsomely never to reveal its secrets.

The room housed my collection. Treasures I'd collected over the years and kept hidden from everyone, but most especially from my father. He hadn't liked us to have attachments to anything, even inanimate objects. No toys or books or games No friends. No pets. Even our mother had been taken from us when we were young, having died after going for a walk along a local trail in the mountains, her body later found at the bottom of a cliff.

My mother hadn't liked hiking—that I remembered about her. So God only knew what she'd been doing on that trail. I'd had my suspicions, but I'd never voiced them. And there had been no point thinking about it. My father had ruled with an iron fist, and fighting him had been a lesson in futility.

A lesson Valentin had never learned, but I'd had to.

I'd had no other option.

The room was blessedly quiet, the non-directional lighting giving it a relaxing glow. Spotlights illuminated special pieces I'd had mounted in climate-controlled cases, plus other, less sensitive items that were no less important.

This was *my* place. *My* things. And I could be as possessive of them as I liked because there was no one to observe me, no one to note how important they were to me and no one to take them away.

Here, in this room, I could allow myself to feel.

I stopped in front of one shelf, looking down at the small green plastic toy soldier illuminated by the spotlight shining on it. An insignificant piece of plastic. Worth nothing.

It had been the first and only toy I'd ever had. A housekeeper, taking pity on me, had given it to me and I'd loved it. I'd played with it every day. Valentin had told me to be careful and not to let our father see, but somehow Papa had found out anyway. He'd tried to force me to throw it in the fire, but Valentin had got hold of it and run away with it, throwing it up onto the roof of our house, where Papa couldn't get it. He'd earned a beating for that.

Valentin had never understood that sometimes it wasn't about the battle but the war. And it had been a war, my childhood. *Our* childhood.

That night I'd had to listen to him trying not to cry in pain, his body bruised from the beating. I'd been so furious with him—that he'd been hurt and all for a ridiculous piece of plastic.

But of course I'd known who'd really been at fault
and it hadn't been Valentin.

He was my older brother by a couple of minutes, and
he'd only been trying to protect me. But the fault had
been mine. If I hadn't taken that toy from the housekeeper, if I hadn't let my father see me playing with it,
then Valentin wouldn't have got hurt.

That was the night I'd decided there was only one
way for us both to survive Domingo's parenting, and it
hadn't been to rebel against him the way Valentin did.
It had been to learn his lessons. Cut off the source of
pain. Our feelings had been weaponised by our father
to hurt us, so the best thing to do was not feel them.

Nothing could matter to me, not even my own
brother.

Eventually I'd retrieved the toy solider and hidden it
under a loose floorboard in my bedroom. I never played
with it again.

'Con?'

The voice that came from behind me was feminine,
light and clear and sweet.

For a moment it felt as if I'd been wandering in a
dark maze, unable to find my out, and suddenly a light
had flickered into life, shining through the darkness,
showing me the way.

My Jenny was here. My Jenny had found me.

Then reality flooded back in—the reality of where
I was and what it meant that she was here.

She'd not only come to the cottage, after I'd ex-
pressly forbidden her to, she'd come into my secret
collection room.

An instinctive territorial anger swept through me, so strong that for a second I couldn't speak. I didn't want to get angry with her, she didn't know how private these things were, how personal, because I'd never told her about my childhood, not any of it. Yet I still felt like an animal whose safe and secret den had been invaded. A dragon whose hoard had been discovered.

She shouldn't be here. She shouldn't be seeing this. All these things were mine and *only* mine.

My hands clenched as I tried to leash the rage, freeze it solid and not let any of it escape, but I could feel it trickling through my fingers.

I needed to get her out of here before I said something I regretted.

I turned sharply.

She stood in the doorway in one of the dresses I'd bought her, this one fitting closely around her breasts before flowing out around her in a waterfall of dusky pink. It was flattering to her curvy figure, the colour warming her skin and making her eyes seem darker and more liquid. Her hair was loose in glossy waves over her shoulders. She'd taken it to wearing it like that because I'd told her I preferred it that way.

The morning sunlight streamed through the windows behind her, catching threads of caramel and toffee in her hair and shining through the material of her dress, illuminating her luscious figure.

She was glowing. She was absolutely beautiful.

I stood frozen, staring at this glowing pink vision. She'd always had the kind of presence that made any room seem lighter and warmer.

'You shouldn't be here.' Anger laced my voice even though I tried to stop it. 'The cottage is forbidden to anyone but me. I told you that.'

Colour stained her cheeks. 'I kn-know. I'm sorry, but—'

'Please leave.'

'Con, I—'

'Get out!' Suddenly I couldn't stand her being there. Couldn't stand the thought of her seeing what was in this room, the evidence of the vulnerable, stunted little boy I'd once been. It felt like a violation. It made me feel ashamed. 'Get out now.'

But she didn't move, and she didn't look anywhere else but at me. She was frowning, her chin taking on that tell-tale stubborn cast. 'No,' she said.

More fury trickled out, and I'd taken a step in her direction before I could stop myself, my grip on my temper loosening. I felt the way I had a few days ago, when she locked the door against me and some part of my brain had exploded with fury. Then, I'd kicked the door down.

This is why you should never have touched her. This is why you should have sent her away. She draws all kinds of emotions out of you and you can't stop her.

She had done even back when she'd been a child, sitting in that chair in my study, swinging her legs and telling me funny stories about the boarding school she'd gone to, making me smile.

I should have known then that she had an ability to touch a part of me no one else had, and I should have guarded myself against her. But she'd been a child, and I'd thought Domingo had killed laughter in me for ever.

I didn't feel like laughing now. My territory had been invaded and I was furious about it.

'Jenny,' I growled, 'you really need to leave.'

She ignored me, her frown deepening as her warm, dark gaze searched my face. 'Are you okay?'

I'd crossed the room before I knew what I was doing, lifted my hands and taken her upper arms in a gentle grip. Her breath caught audibly. There were dark circles beneath her eyes, as if she hadn't slept well.

What are you doing? Why are you manhandling her? She's Jenny...she's your *Jenny. Remember what happened to Domingo. Remember what you did.*

I couldn't move. She felt breakable in my hands, fragile as a china shepherdess. I'd already lost control with her once before, and now here I was, laying hands on her again...

She was still frowning, looking up at me, and yet there was no fear in her lovely face, only a concern that gripped me by the throat.

She shouldn't be concerned for me. Not when I hadn't shown any concern for her.

'I know you don't want me in here, and I'm sorry,' she said. 'I didn't mean to intrude. But...you've been gone all day and I... I was worried for you.'

I struggled to contain my anger, to keep it locked down. She had intruded into my private space, but not so she could discover my secrets and use them against me.

She'd been worried about me.

'You don't need to worry,' I said through gritted teeth. 'I'm fine.'

CHAPTER THIRTEEN

Jenny

HE DIDN'T WANT me here, and if the look of fury that had momentarily crossed his face when I'd stepped into the room hadn't been enough of a sign, then the tension radiating through every line of his body and the fierce heat in his black eyes certainly was.

He wasn't fine. He wasn't fine at all. He was furiously angry. And now, of course, I wanted to know why.

I also wanted to know why he was always gone when I woke up in the mornings, and why he stayed here in the cottage the entire day. Why he only came back in the evenings, and why he'd then take me to bed and keep me there until dinner time.

And, most importantly, I wanted to know why he wouldn't talk to me. Because we hadn't discussed the wedding, or when we'd return to London, or what would happen after that. He'd told me he'd instructed one of his staff members to tell my mother where I was, and to contact the shelter where I worked. But we hadn't discussed anything beyond that. We hadn't discussed anything at all.

Those first few days I'd been too dazed and a little drunk with the effects of sex to notice the distance he'd put between us. But then, as the fifth day came around and he'd left me alone, I'd had enough. I couldn't let this distance between us continue, not when we were going to be married and had a child to raise together.

So I'd crossed the rolling green lawns to his cottage. If it had only been about myself, maybe I'd have left him to his privacy, but it wasn't only about me. It was about the baby, too. I couldn't let him dictate everything. I couldn't let him walk all over me.

I had to make a stand.

His stare was fierce, his heat surrounding me. He was in a white shirt and charcoal-grey trousers, the stark colours highlighting his dark beauty, a perfect foil to the rage burning in his obsidian eyes.

'Don't be ridiculous,' I said, ignoring the hard grip he had on my arms. 'You're not fine. If you were fine you wouldn't have been skulking in this cottage for the past five days.'

It was an unwise thing to say, but someone had to say it to him. And since I was apparently the only person who wasn't afraid of him, that someone had to be me.

He stared at me for one long second, then muttered a curse under his breath and let me go, stepping away, withdrawing his heat. A chill crept through me at the loss of his warmth. I tried to ignore it.

The ice was back in his eyes, the fierce expression fading, his perfect features hardening.

I didn't like it. I preferred his anger to his cold detachment, because at least that was honest. At least that was more him than this ice was.

'In there,' he said curtly, nodding his head in the direction of the office.

Shoving away the feeling of disappointment, I turned and stepped back through the doorway, leaving him to shut the door on that fascinating secret room. A wall of shelves slid back into place, and I had to bite down on my urge to ask him what was in there, because I hadn't looked when I'd had the chance. Not when all I'd seen was him.

Once the shelves were back, Con came over to me and slid a hand beneath my elbow, guiding me over to a couch and sitting me down on it.

The tiny cottage had been converted into a large, comfortable office, with that big desk and lots of shelving. The wooden floor was very old, dark and pitted, yet gleaming. A few hand-knotted silk rugs covered it, and under the window opposite the desk was the comfortable-looking couch in dark leather. The walls were undressed stone and very thick, giving the place a cosy, contained and secure atmosphere.

Con folded his arms over his broad chest, looming over me, staring at me with those cold eyes.

I was beginning to hate that expression, the one he showed to everyone else. Didn't he know he didn't need to be that way with me? Didn't he know he could be himself when he was with me?

Abruptly, I felt close to tears, though I wasn't sure why. Perhaps it was the way he'd turned on me, because, regardless of whether I'd invaded his privacy or not, I hadn't expected that. He'd never been angry with me before, yet in the space of the past five days cold and angry was all he seemed to be.

It didn't start five days ago, and you know it.

That was true. He'd been cold and distant ever since I'd left Spain to live in London. Apart from that night in the garden, when we'd both crossed a line we hadn't been able to come back from.

And then you both broke what you'd once had. You broke it irretrievably.

Maybe. But I suspected something had broken before that night. And I still didn't know what it was, because he wouldn't tell me.

I bit my lip hard, shoving away the tears and reaching for anger instead. 'What was all that about?' I demanded.

'What was what about?'

'You, in that room. Getting so angry with me.'

A muscle ticked in the side of his hard jaw. 'I don't want to talk about it.'

'Okay, fine. So is that how it's going to be? Our marriage? Sex whenever you want it and then you disappearing off God knows where and refusing to talk to me?'

His dark brows twitched. 'What more do you want?'

'I want you to be there!' The words came out far more vehemently than I'd expected, and I tried to moderate my tone. 'I don't want this distance you keep putting between us. I don't understand it, not when we have so much we need to talk about.'

Something flickered behind his cold black eyes, a glimpse of an emotion I couldn't read. 'Fine. Let us talk about the arrangements now.'

His voice was expressionless, blank as a stone wall.

It made me even angrier.

'I don't want to talk about the "arrangements",' I snapped. 'I want to talk about why, for the past five days, you've done nothing but have sex with me and leave.'

The muscle in his jaw leapt again. 'I have work I need to do.'

'You ignored me, Con,' I said flatly. 'Funny how you were able to work years ago in your office and you didn't mind talking to me then.'

The ice in his expression cracked, another emotion I couldn't name flickering across his beautiful face. He turned abruptly and strode over to the desk, looking down at the stack of papers neatly piled on top of it. 'I told you that sex was all I could give you, Jenny. I meant it.'

I stared at his tall figure, his broad shoulders rigid with tension, and part of me wanted to go to him and put my arms around him. But I was also angry, and I couldn't give in to the need to make him feel better, not all the time. Not if I wanted to close this distance between us.

Because it wasn't a physical distance, it was emotional. He was pulling away from me and, sure, he'd told me he couldn't give me love, but he could at least be the friend he'd once been to me. Couldn't we go back to that? Didn't I deserve that? Didn't our baby? What if he pulled away from our child? Would he put this distance between them too?

'What happened to being my friend?' I asked, my hands tightly clasped in my lap. 'You can't be that either?'

There was a long silence.

'No,' he said.

A cold current of shock rippled through me.

Are you really that surprised? He hasn't been a friend to you since you left Madrid.

'Why not?' I asked hoarsely. 'You never told me why you cut me off. Was it me? Did I do something? Con, I—'

'No.' He glanced at me all of a sudden, his gaze fierce. 'It's nothing you did. It's not your fault.'

I felt bewildered. 'Then…why?'

He looked back down at the stack of papers and placed one hand carefully on top of them, as if to protect them from a non-existent wind. 'I never spoke to you about my childhood, did I? I never talked about Domingo.'

As soon as he said the words, a knowledge that had always been there twisted deep inside me. He had always been tense when his father had been around, always cold, detached. And, no, he'd never spoken about Domingo, or the twin brother he'd lost at seventeen.

There is probably a reason for that.

'No, you didn't,' I said softly.

'I did not want you to know. I did not want it to… touch you.'

Foreboding gripped me. Domingo hadn't been an

easy man, and he certainly hadn't liked me. I'd tried my best to be a good stepdaughter, but he'd avoided me for some reason.

'What did he do to you, Con?' I whispered.

'It's better if you don't know.' His voice was completely expressionless. 'Suffice to say that I decided long ago it was better for me not to form any…emotional attachments.'

I blinked, taken aback. Then immediately I wanted to know why he'd decided that and what had made him choose something so extreme? But I knew from the look on his face that he wasn't going to tell me.

So instead I said, 'Is that why you said you couldn't give me love?'

'Yes.'

'But…you were my friend before,' I pointed out. 'What changed? Because something did.'

He turned his head, his black gaze pinning me to the couch where I sat. 'You did, Jenny. It changed because of you.'

A cold little shock pulsed through me. 'What do you mean?'

'Did you never wonder why, for the past four years, I never visited you? Never called you? Never replied to your emails or texts?'

'Of course I wondered.' My voice had gone hoarse. 'I wondered all the time.'

'It was because I wanted you.'

I sat on the couch, my heartbeat loud in my ears, four years of silence shifting and altering and finally falling into place. 'And you were…what? Keeping your distance?' My voice sounded faint and slightly cracked.

'Yes, I was keeping my distance.' His gaze burned. 'I was too old for you, and you were my friend, my step-sister. My duty was and still is to protect you, most especially from myself.'

It made sense, so much sense. The years of curt, cold messages, and finally no messages at all. And then that night in the garden, how he'd fallen on me like a beast let out of a cage…

I swallowed, the cold shock slowly fading to be replaced by heat.

He'd wanted me all those years. He'd wanted me the way I'd wanted him.

'But you don't need to protect me any more,' I said. 'You can—'

'Yes, I do,' he interrupted. 'And it's even more important now. You don't want a platonic marriage, Jenny, so I can promise you that it won't be. And if you want to talk about our living arrangements, our wedding, how we will raise our child, then we will. We can organise all of that together. It will not be an issue. But I cannot be your friend again. The relationship we once had is over.'

Tears prickled once again, loss throbbing behind my breastbone. But I ignored the sensations. Because all of this was *his* decision, not mine. He was the one who'd decided on distance, who'd thought he had to 'protect' me, or some such nonsense. Who now seemed to think that sex was an adequate replacement for his friendship.

Even though the sex was very good indeed, I discovered that I'd been right. It *wasn't* enough.

I wanted him. And it wasn't only about me, it was about our baby as well.

'What about our child, Con?' I asked flatly. 'Will you distance yourself from them too? Will you tell them that you can't give them love?'

That muscle in the side of his jaw jerked and jerked again. 'That's not—'

'How do you think they'll feel when they say *I love you, Daddy* and you don't say it back?'

CHAPTER FOURTEEN

Constantine

THE WORDS HUNG in the air, the sharp edges of them glittering like knives.

I turned away from her, looked back down at the papers on my desk, struggling to contain the fury and anguish twisting deep inside me.

I love you, Daddy. They were words I'd said once to my own father, back when I was very young. Too young to know yet how painful those emotions could be.

Domingo had laughed. 'You really are a stupid boy, aren't you?' he'd said. 'You should be more like your brother. He doesn't bother with any of that nonsense.'

That had been the start of the wedge he'd driven between Valentin and I. Valentin had been rebellious, confrontational. Never doing what Papa said and constantly fighting with him. While I... I had found such confrontations distressing. They'd been painful and I'd hated conflict.

I had been weak back then. Vulnerable. I still remembered the cruel edge to his laugh and the lazy amusement on his face as he'd called me stupid. Reducing my feelings to something shameful and humiliating.

The only way to protect myself from him had been to become him, and I couldn't allow the same thing to happen to any child of mine.

I would never intentionally do anything to hurt them the way Papa had hurt me, but if I was finding it difficult to control my feelings around Jenny, then controlling my feelings around my child was going to be impossible.

How could I expose them to that? I couldn't trust myself.

'I will tell them the truth,' I bit out. 'That I will protect them with everything I have, but love is something they will only be able to get from their mother.'

'Oh, Con...' Jenny didn't sound angry now, her voice full of a compassion that made me ache. 'What happened to you?'

Unconsciously I closed the hand resting on top of the papers into a fist.

She was still on the couch, her hands clasped in her lap, the sunlight from the window behind her streaming in, making her glow, illuminating all the dark spaces in the cottage.

Illuminating all the dark spaces in my heart, too.

I'd told her the truth, that I hadn't wanted her to know about the war zone that had been my childhood. I hadn't wanted any of that to touch her. I'd wanted her to stay the bright light that I turned to when things were dark.

I'd thought I'd never have to tell her, and yet... I couldn't keep it from her, not now. Not when we were going to be married and would have a child to bring up. It wasn't fair to her, and it wasn't fair to our child either.

Both my hands were now clenched tightly, and no matter how hard I tried to relax them, they wouldn't.

'What happened to me?' I echoed, my voice sounding strange and hollow in the silence of the cottage. 'Domingo was a psychopath, Jenny. You wouldn't have known, because he hid it well, but he was a smiling, charming psychopath. So I suppose you could say that what happened to me was him.'

'A psychopath?' The words were a soft, scraped whisper as horror rippled over her lovely face. 'Con…'

I looked away, unable to bear her expression, staring down at the dark wood of my desk. 'I think Catherine sent you away to school because she didn't want you anywhere near him and with good reason. My childhood was a war zone. Domingo wouldn't allow Valentin and I any kind of attachments. Not to anything.'

I wanted the words to be flat and toneless, the facts issued and nothing but. Yet anger tinged them no matter how hard I tried to prevent it.

'We had no toys. No friends. No pets. We only had each other, and Domingo would use that bond against us. He would manipulate us, turn us against each other. Valentin responded with argument and rebellion, while I…' I took a breath. 'It seemed safer not to feel anything at all.'

There was a long, shocked silence.

I didn't want to look at her. I didn't want to see what was on her lovely face. Deep down, I'd thought that now Domingo was gone his poison would have gone with him, but it hadn't. It was reaching beyond the grave and now it was touching Jenny. My Jenny.

That was my fault. I poisoned everything I touched, too.

I needed to get out of the cottage, away from her gentle presence, away from the consequences of my own actions just for once.

I turned from the desk, ready to stride out, only to have warm arms wrap themselves around me and soft curves press against my chest. Jenny looked up at me, her dark eyes liquid with tears, with sympathy, and a compassion that made my entire being clench tight.

I went rigid in her grip, but she didn't let me go, softness and heat to the sharp edges and ice inside of me.

'She kept me safe,' Jenny said thickly. 'But who kept you safe? Who, Con?'

We both knew the answer to that, and when I didn't speak she pressed her face to my chest and held me tight, as if her embrace would ease the toxic mixture of emotion inside me.

And it did. I felt the moment all the rage and pain I'd turned inward shift, the press of feminine curves altering it, turning it into a volcano of something hotter, more intense, and far more welcome.

Desire leapt high, consuming me, and for a second all I could do was stand there in a futile attempt to take control.

But there was no controlling it. My hands were in her hair before I could stop myself, pulling her head away from my chest, turning her delicate face up so I could bend and take her mouth like a man possessed.

She didn't pull away and she didn't stop me. Her arms tightened and she went up on her toes, kissing me back as hungrily as I was kissing her.

Her mouth was hot and sweet and generous, just like her soul, and I clenched my hands tightly in her hair, holding her fast as I gorged myself on her, letting the taste of her flood through me, blotting out all the rage and pain I'd told myself I didn't feel.

She held nothing back, giving me everything, and I took it. I couldn't stop.

I lifted my mouth from hers only so I could tear her pretty pink dress from her body, and then her pretty pink underwear too. Her fingers fumbled with my shirt buttons, pulling at them as if she was as desperate for that skin-on-skin contact as I was.

I helped her, getting rid of my shirt and then dealing with my trousers and the rest of my clothing, wanting nothing more than to be rid of any constraints. Then, naked, I picked her up in my arms and took her over to the couch, laying her on the cushions before following her down and pinning her beneath me.

Her hair was in wild curls over the cushions and tangled over her shoulders, her face flushed. Her eyes were liquid and there were tear tracks on her cheeks. I bent and kissed away the tears, drowning myself in the taste of salt and the sweetness of her skin before finding her mouth again and kissing her deeply and with hunger.

She tasted of summer and sunlight, champagne and strawberries. Of long, warm twilights and perfumed rose gardens. Of all the fantasies I'd ever had about her. I couldn't get enough. The scent of her arousal was driving me mad.

I kissed my way down her throat to the curve of her breasts, flicking my tongue over her nipple, licking her, teasing her. Then I drew the hard bud into my mouth and sucked. She gasped, arching into me, her hands gripping my shoulders.

She tasted delicious. I wanted to spend time feasting on her, but my own needs were becoming too much for me to control. I shifted between her soft thighs, easing the hard length of my shaft through the hot, wet folds of her sex, feeling her shudder against me.

She whispered my name and then, as I nipped the sensitive bud of her nipple, she groaned aloud.

I was losing myself in the taste of her, the sound of her gasps and the feel of her heat, and all I wanted to do was lose myself more, get rid of all the emotion inside me and leave nothing behind but pleasure.

I moved again, holding her hips as I positioned myself, then pushed into her, a groan escaping me at the feel of her hot flesh parting around mine, only to grip me tight, holding me inside her. Welcoming me. She was slick and tight and perfect. I slid my hands beneath the softness of her rear, tilting her so I could go deeper, making both of us gasp.

Then I was moving, unable to stop, my mouth on hers, kissing her harder as I moved inside her, a relentless and intoxicating pleasure driving me on.

Her nails dug into my shoulders and I relished it, glorying in how she could be as demanding as I was, her passion burning hot and strong.

I poured myself into her, all my pain and my rage, and she took it and changed it, giving me back only ecstasy and heat and wild passion.

It was magic. It was like nothing I'd ever had from anyone in my entire life. It was too much.

I slipped my hand down between her thighs, giving her back what I could before all conscious thought left me and I was driving myself deep into her, hard and fast, feeling her convulse around me as the climax took her and she screamed my name.

And then I followed, annihilated by the pleasure that swept over me with all the force of a tidal wave, knocking me over and pulling me under.

CHAPTER FIFTEEN

Jenny

I LAY BENEATH HIM, parts of me utterly shattered while other parts of me were hungry for more. And yet my heart ached.

He'd lowered his head, his face turned against my neck, his warm breath ghosting over my skin. He was a heavy weight on me, pinning me to the couch, but I didn't mind it. I never had. Beneath him I felt safe and secure, as if he was sheltering me from the world.

Except…who sheltered him? Had he ever had anyone? Had he ever had someone who'd brought him the same kind of solace and understanding he'd brought me? I had tried, but from what he'd said about his childhood I knew it hadn't been enough.

I ran my fingers through his short, thick black hair. It felt like raw silk against my skin. My body might feel utterly sated, but inside I hurt.

I hurt for him.

I'd always wondered why my mother had sent me away to boarding school, and I'd assumed it was be-

cause she hadn't wanted me around. I hadn't realised—
and why would I?—that she'd sent me away to protect
me from Domingo.

That made sense, given what I now knew about him.
But my safety paled in comparison to the realisation of
what it had meant for Constantine.

His father had been a psychopath, using him and his
brother. Using their bond to hurt them and manipulate
them. And all the while denying them all the things a
child needed in order to grow.

No friends. No pets. Not even any toys.

I couldn't imagine it. It horrified me to my core. Yet
it also explained things. Con had said it was safer for
him not to feel anything at all, and I could see now why
he thought that. Why he'd always been so distant and so
cold. Why it had always seemed as if he was armour-
ing himself. Because he had been. He'd been armour-
ing himself against his father.

I'd stayed out of Domingo's way, mostly, but whenever I'd noticed Con getting very tense around him,
I'd tried my best to distract him. Domingo had never
responded to my attempts to befriend him, shaking
me off as if I was insect and walking away. I'd never
discovered why I'd made him so uncomfortable, yet I
felt pleased about it now. If only I'd known at the time
I would have tried even harder to make sure Domingo
stayed away.

Con had relaxed, his big body covering me like a
heavy warm blanket. All the tension from before had
bled out of him and now he lay on me unmoving.

Out of his suit he was a glorious specimen of manhood. Wide shoulders, broad chest and chiselled abs, all that muscled power covered with smooth, velvety olive skin.

Touching him was a delight and I didn't deny myself, dropping my hand from his hair to stroke down his back.

'I'm sorry.' My voice sounded thick in the heavy silence. 'I'm so sorry you had such a dreadful childhood.' It was a useless thing to say, but I couldn't think of anything else. And I wanted him to know that I felt for him.

He let out a long breath, its warmth chasing over my skin, and I thought he might move. Might cover himself in ice, detach himself once again. But he didn't.

'You do not know how much I valued your friendship, Jenny Grey,' he murmured. 'You were the first friend I ever had.'

Tears rose in my eyes at the realisation of what that must have meant for him. 'I was?' I asked shakily.

'Yes.' And then, as I was recovering from that, he added, almost casually, 'Valentin has come back.'

I went still. 'What? No, Valentin's dead. You told me that—'

'He's not dead.'

Slowly, Constantine lifted his head and looked down at me, his eyes full of some complicated emotion I couldn't read.

'That night in the garden, when you found me, I'd had a call from a source informing me that he was alive, that he hadn't died in a car crash after all.'

I stared at him in shock. 'I don't understand. If he's not dead, then what happened to him?'

'It looks like he spent a few years in hiding—my sources weren't able to tell me where—before appearing suddenly as the head of a multi-million-dollar security firm.' He reached for one of my curls, winding it slowly around one finger. 'You wanted to know why the power went out that night in the mansion last week? It was Valentin. He created a...disturbance. He kidnapped Olivia.'

More shock pulsed through me. The lights had gone out as I'd waited for Constantine in that room. And then he'd appeared, telling me he was going to marry me. That he'd changed his mind about Olivia.

But he hadn't changed his mind. He'd decided to marry me because his twin brother had come back from the dead and taken Olivia.

'Oh, my God...' I breathed, struggling suddenly to sit up. 'He kidnapped her...? Then what are you doing—?'

'Be still,' Con said quietly, not moving an inch, holding me down on the couch with the weight of his body. 'Valentin won't hurt her, though she might very well hurt him. He's told me he's going to take the company from me, but I don't think it's Silver Inc he actually wants. I think it's Olivia.'

I was still trying to process what he'd said, my heartbeat racing. 'Why didn't you tell me?'

He let go of the lock of hair he'd been playing with, brushing his fingers carefully over my collarbone, his touch making me shiver. 'I didn't want you to know. I didn't want anyone to know. Not until I'd decided how

I was going to deal with the situation.' His gaze flicked to mine. 'He's in the Maldives at present, with Olivia.'

It was…a lot. Everything he'd just told me was a lot. Firstly that his father had been an abusive monster, and then that the twin brother he'd thought dead was very much alive and now with his erstwhile fiancée. Not to mention the fact that he'd kept all of this secret from me.

I wasn't sure of what to say. 'Have you…spoken to him?'

Con shook his head. 'He keeps leaving messages for me, but I haven't responded.'

'Why not? Aren't you pleased that he's not dead?'

His stroking fingers descended lower, tracing the curve of my breast, his attention on what he was doing. 'That's an interesting question,' he murmured.

I shoved away the delicious prickle over my skin that his touch drew, concentrating instead on his beautiful face, trying to read him. There were emotions there, deep and strong, but untangling them was difficult. Then again, I'd had years of watching his face. Years of seeing beneath his cold detachment—which I understood the reason for now—to the volcanic heart of him. And I could hear the thread that ran through his voice, that coloured every word.

'You're angry with him,' I said softly. 'You're furious.'

He flashed me one hot black look and, yes, I was right. The fury that I'd seen before, that had been in his every movement as he'd taken me on the couch, was there, starkly burning in every line of his perfect features.

'He let me think he was dead,' Con said, his lilting Spanish accent turning every word into angry poetry. 'He left me alone with that monster for fifteen years. And he never contacted me, not once.' His mouth was hard. 'He made our lives a misery, Jenny. His constant rebellions, his resistance to our father's rules, made everything worse. If he'd only done what Papa had said, even once. If he'd—' Con broke off, glancing back down at his fingers, still stroking the curve of my breast. 'I had a plastic toy soldier, given to me by a housekeeper. It was the only toy I'd ever had and I loved it. Valentin told me I had to be careful with it, that I couldn't let our father see me with it. But I didn't listen. Papa found out and he was angry. He tried to make me burn it in the fire, but Valentin took it and threw it on the roof so Papa couldn't get it.'

I lay there very still, my gaze fixed on his face, not daring to breathe in case he stopped talking.

'That enraged Domingo. He beat Valentin badly for disobeying him.' Con let out a breath. 'Valentin took the beating intended for me and… Papa broke his ribs.'

An anguished sound escaped before I could stop it, the horror of it settling inside me. But Con didn't look up, too lost in his terrible memories.

'I shouldn't be angry with him,' he went on after a moment. 'Not when all of it was my fault. I should not have accepted the toy and I should have listened to Valentin when he told me to be careful with it. I should not have let my father see it.' He paused. 'I should have put it in the fire. If I had it would have been one less beating Valentin took for me. But…'

He didn't need to go on. I could already see why he hadn't wanted to give up his toy. He'd had nothing, so a plastic toy soldier must have seemed worth the risk. Yet it had ended up with his brother being beaten.

I ached for him. He was a man who felt deeply, I already knew that, and I suspected that as boy he must have been the same. A loving boy who'd had to protect himself in any way he could. And he'd cut himself off from his emotions so completely he didn't feel anything at all.

Yet that boy was still there, beneath all that ice. He'd looked after a nest of chicks for an eleven-year-old girl and had always remembered to send her postcards from all the countries he'd been to. He'd given her a birthday card when everyone else had forgotten and he'd listened to her chatter inanely, and he'd always taken her seriously. He'd never judged her, and he'd never criticised her. He'd made her feel that she wasn't alone.

But that loving boy had lost the only person he'd ever loved and who'd ever loved him. The brother who'd left him alone with a father who'd twisted him into something he never should have been.

No wonder he was so lonely.

I'd never developed the hard callus my mother had. I'd never been able to hide my own loneliness away. My mother had channelled hers into an endless succession of men who didn't love her and whom she didn't love. But I couldn't do that. Just as I couldn't do what Con had done, cutting himself off from his emotions completely.

I'd always thought that feeling so deeply was a weakness in me somehow, a flaw. Yet it didn't feel like a flaw now. Now, looking at Con and the anguish I saw deep inside him, it felt like a gift I could give him. He'd forgotten how to feel, how to process emotions, so they were harsh and jagged and painful inside him. But I could help. Whether he wanted my friendship or not, he needed it.

He needed to talk to someone he could trust.

I was that someone.

'Years ago,' I said huskily, 'I told you that I was your friend.'

He glanced up at me and this time I couldn't read his expression at all, his black eyes fathomless. He didn't speak, only stared at me.

'I'm still your friend, Con. You don't need to distance yourself. You don't need to protect me. I know you. I have known you since I was a child, and there is nothing in you that scares me. You can trust me. I'm here for you. I always have been.'

He said nothing for a long moment. Then abruptly he leaned down and brushed his mouth over mine in a featherlight kiss.

I dug my fingers into the hard muscle of his shoulders, wanting more, but he didn't deepen it, only lifted his head, staring down into my eyes. His hand curved over my stomach, where our baby grew. 'I will not hurt our child,' he said, with all the certainty of a vow. 'I became like Domingo in order to survive, but I will never be like him as a father. Never.'

'I know,' I said simply. 'And you're not him. You never were.'

His hand was large and warm, resting on my stomach.

'You're going to make a wonderful mother, Jenny. I couldn't ask for a better mother for my children.'

A flush of heat went through me, my whole being responding to his praise like a flower opening its petals to the sun. I felt as if I was back in his study and he was telling me very seriously that my mother didn't know what she was talking about and that if I wanted to try for med school I should, because I had both the intelligence and the work ethic.

'I don't know…' I felt oddly hesitant. 'I didn't have the best role model for a mother. I have no idea of how or what you're supposed to do, or…or anything, really.'

They were fears I'd had, but never wanted to acknowledge. That for all my determination to provide a stable and secure home for my child, I wouldn't be able to.

There had been so many things I'd wanted to do, and I'd never succeeded at any of them, so how was I supposed to succeed at this?

'Does anyone the first time they become a parent?' His hand lifted and cupped my cheek, his thumb brushing over my cheekbone. 'You're beautiful, you're successful, you're—'

I snorted. 'I'm not successful.'

'You are,' he insisted. 'You wanted to work with charities and that's exactly what you're doing. Isn't that success? Working in a job that makes you happy and fulfils you?'

'I suppose so.' I sighed. 'I never got into med school, though.'

'So?' One imperious black brow rose. 'You can try

again, you know. Plenty of people go back to university years after they leave school.'

I rolled my eyes and gave his shoulder a little push. 'That's not the point.'

He ignored the push. 'Then what is?'

'You know… I think I'm just unsure. I badly want to be a better mother than mine was. I want to give our child the best start in life that I can.'

Something in his hard face softened, his beautiful mouth curving. 'And you will. You already know what *not* to do, correct?'

'True.'

'And, apart from that, you're warm, you're empathetic, you're giving. And you care. You have so much love to give our baby, Jenny. You will be the best mother a child could have.'

There was so much conviction in his voice that my throat closed with emotion. He'd always had the ability to make me feel better about myself. Always.

'Thank you,' I said huskily, reaching out to touch his face. 'That means a lot to me.' Then, to lighten the atmosphere, because I didn't want to cry, I said, 'She always thought I should marry you. That since she had Domingo I should get in there and snag you.'

It was a risk to tease him with that, because I had no idea how he'd take it. I hoped he'd understand that it wasn't something I'd ever have done, but who knew?

Yet his dark eyes glittered with amusement, the lines around his hard, carved mouth relaxing. 'Well, you did snag me, didn't you?' He shifted against me. 'And now that you have, what are you going to do with me?'

My heart fluttered. I'd thought I'd lost the ability to make him smile and, while it wasn't quite like the smiles he'd used to give me, the potential was there.

'I suppose I have a few options.' I lifted a hand to his broad shoulder, stroking it then trailing my fingers down his hard, carved chest. 'I could try seducing you.'

'That's true,' he agreed. 'You could try. But I warn you: I'm rather difficult to seduce.'

My heart fluttered even harder. Oh, yes, that was definitely amusement. 'No, you're not.'

One corner of his mouth turned up and my heart turned over. 'Prove it, then.'

So, I did.

CHAPTER SIXTEEN

Constantine

I WOKE EARLY the next morning, coming to consciousness instantly, a warm and very naked female body in my arms. I was hard, and all I could think about was waking her up then putting her on her back and sinking inside the tight, wet heat of her body.

But she was sleeping peacefully, and I had kept her up late the night before, so instead I raised myself on an elbow and allowed myself the total indulgence of gazing down at her, studying her sleeping face.

She looked so young, her soft rose petal skin pink with warmth, her features relaxed in sleep. Her eyelashes were thick, and darker than the hair on her head, a sable colour that looked just as soft to the touch as the rest of her. Her nose was slightly upturned, and her mouth was full and delightfully sensual.

She was beautiful. I knew she felt that she didn't have her mother's looks, but she did. Catherine's beauty was cold and hard-edged—a bit like Olivia's—but Jenny's was different. Jenny's was soft, and had a deep and generous sensuality that both Catherine and Olivia had lacked. Or at least when it came to Olivia I hadn't seen it.

But I saw Jenny's. It came from the deep well of empathy inside her, her warm, unselfish spirit. She was a giving person—she'd always had been, ever since she'd turned up that day in the mansion and declared that she was going to be my friend.

I touched her cheek very lightly, her skin satin-smooth beneath my finger.

I hadn't wanted to tell her about Domingo and my childhood, yet now I had I couldn't bring myself to regret it. It felt as if a weight had been lifted from my shoulders, a weight I hadn't realised I'd been carrying. Even telling her about Valentin and his return had been…good.

She hadn't been angry with me for not telling her. She hadn't turned it into a battle. She hadn't used the confession to get something out of me, and she hadn't pressed for any more information than I'd been willing to give her.

She'd simply let me talk, her fingers playing with my hair and stroking my back as I lay on her warm body. I should have moved to make her more comfortable, since I was heavy, but she hadn't insisted and so I hadn't moved. She was wonderful to lie against. She was soft and she smelled like heaven.

You trust her.

Perhaps it shouldn't have been so surprising. I wouldn't have told her everything if I hadn't trusted her on some level.

'You can trust me. I'm here for you. I always have been.'

Her words from the day before echoed in my head, along with the conviction I'd seen in her dark eyes.

She *had* always been there for me. But I hadn't been there for her, had I? I'd cut her off for four years, kept myself emotionally distant from her without an explanation. Then I'd told her yesterday that we could never go back to being friends and she'd looked so stricken…

A tight feeling coiled in my chest and I stroked the side of her cheek.

I couldn't keep doing that to her. I couldn't keep holding myself apart. Every decision I'd made for the past four years had hurt her, and that wasn't fair.

Telling her about the night Valentin had left, when I'd lost my temper, going to Domingo in a rage, was impossible. That she must never know. But surely I didn't have to keep the rest of it from her. Surely I could stay being her friend. As she'd said, we'd managed it before. And, while things were different now, I didn't see why we couldn't manage it again.

I could stay in control of myself, and while she might be vulnerable, she also had that thread of pure steel running through her.

It fascinated me how she could be so open and yet so strong. As if the emotions she wore so honestly were a strength and an armour in themselves, not a weakness that could be exploited and weaponised.

She stirred, giving a sigh, and those long, silky eyelashes of hers fluttered, then lifted. Her eyes were such a warm brown, like hot chocolate, and when she smiled, as she did now, I swore I could see rays of sunshine dancing in them.

'Good morning,' she murmured sleepily, a pink flush spreading over her skin. 'Exactly how long have you been lying there watching me?'

'I'm not sure.' My fingers trailed over her jaw and down the side of her neck. 'Does it disturb you?'

'No.' She put her hand on my chest, her touch warm on my bare skin. 'Though I didn't realise I was quite so fascinating.'

'You are.' I looked down into her eyes. 'How do you do it, Jenny? How do you walk around with your emotions so close to the surface? So everyone can see exactly what you're feeling? Aren't you afraid?'

Her brow furrowed. 'Afraid of what?'

'Afraid someone will take advantage of you.'

'Well, I didn't have the kind of childhood you had so, no, that has never been my first thought. Though Mum was always telling me I was too soft for my own good, that I needed to be colder, more calculating.' Her fingers brushed over my chest in a gentle caress. 'I just… couldn't. It felt dishonest and wrong.' Her gaze flicked up to meet mine. 'She uses men, you know. Manipulates their emotions in order to get access to their money. In fact, now I think about it, she's more than a little like your father.'

I, too, had thought that. The two of them had seemed well suited. And that made Jenny all the more fascinating. Because while I had tried to make myself like my father, she had done the opposite. She had rebelled.

Like Val. And you always had a sneaking admiration for him.

Yes, that was true. Part of me had loved his blatant opposition. Loved how it had enraged our cold father. It just hadn't been my choice.

I frowned with a sudden suspicion. 'Did Catherine ever hurt you? Did she ever try to make you—?'

'No,' Jenny murmured firmly, pressing her fingers against my chest as if to emphasise the word. 'No, she didn't. But you know she was never very…loving. She didn't even seem to like me all that much. I used to wonder sometimes if it was because I wasn't planned, and because my father left her when she found out she was pregnant with me.' Her gaze dropped from mine, her attention on her hand. 'There were a few times I wanted to ask her why she didn't just get rid of me, but I… I never had the courage.' Jenny let out a soft breath. 'I think I was afraid of the answer.'

I hadn't really thought Catherine would have hurt Jenny physically, but I knew she'd hurt her emotionally… that her treatment as a child had left scars. That they weren't quite as dark as the ones that my father had left on me didn't matter. What mattered was the pain they'd left, and the fact that I could do something about it.

I had been working hard at Silver Inc, trying to change the culture of fear Domingo had instituted, but sometimes I feared that the damage he'd done was beyond repair. He'd destroyed the few relationships I'd had, after all.

Yet while Valentin was lost to me, Jenny wasn't.

'Anyway,' Jenny went on quietly, 'she thought I

should marry you. That I was stupid for wanting to work at a charity when I could simply seduce you and be your wife.'

Shouldn't you not *be discussing this? What happened to emotional distance?*

No, I couldn't do love, but I could certainly do friendship. I could certainly do reassurance. And for Jenny I would do just about anything. Besides, apart from anything else, no one had needed me before, and I wanted to hold on to that feeling for as long as I could.

'Simply seduce me, hmm?' I murmured, amused despite myself. I wasn't angry at the confession. 'Sounds easy.'

She gave me a teasing look from underneath her lashes. 'It was yesterday.'

I liked how she flirted with me, yet I had a sense that there was more going on, that she wasn't telling me quite everything.

I reached down and slid a finger beneath her chin, tilting her face up so I could see her, and caught the doubt that flickered in the depths of her deep brown eyes. 'There's more, though, isn't there?' I said softly. 'Tell me what worries you.'

'A lot of things.' She paused and swallowed. 'I want to give our child safety and security and stability, like I told you. But this baby wasn't planned, and I know you wouldn't ever have married me if I wasn't pregnant. I just worry that I'm not…successful enough to be your wife. That one day you'll see it and…' Her voice had gone husky. 'I don't want you to be disappointed in me and I don't want you to regret marrying me.'

My chest tightened, an ache sitting behind my breast-bone. Because I understood. Her childhood had been chaotic and lonely, and of course she wouldn't want that for our child—I didn't want that for our child myself.

'You won't disappoint me,' I said huskily. 'It's impossible. You were the one bright spot in my life. The only good thing. You never lied to me or tried to manipulate me. You distracted me when I needed it and you made me smile. You always cared, Jenny. You always cared so much. So why would I *ever* regret marrying you?'

Her eyes filled with tears. 'Don't make me cry, you horrible man. I swore I would never cry in front of you again.'

Ah, yes, that night in the garden. When she'd told me she loved me and I'd said those awful things to her. She'd cried, and even though I'd tried to tell myself I felt nothing, in breaking her I'd broken a part of myself, too.

I stroked her cheek with my thumb, then bent and kissed away the tears. 'I'm sorry.' They weren't words I said often, if at all, but if anyone deserved them it was her. 'I'm sorry for the way I've treated you for the past four years, for cutting you off without explanation. And I'm sorry for what I said to you that night. You didn't deserve it—not any of it. The only excuse I can give was that it was the day when I'd found out Valentin was alive, and I was…not myself.'

Her fingers spread on my chest, a soft warmth sitting on my skin. The endless well of compassion and sympathy that was Jenny's spirit glowed in her eyes.

And what have you done to deserve it? Nothing. You've done nothing.

I hadn't. I'd forced her to come to Scotland with me. Forced her into accepting marriage. I'd seduced her and then shut her out. Shouted at her. Kicked down her door. I'd been a bastard, and yet all I could see in her eyes was forgiveness.

'I know you weren't,' she said. 'It made me angry with you for months, but even back then I knew something was wrong. It makes sense now.'

I could feel it twist inside me then, the need to tell her everything. The one thing I'd left out, that I'd let fester inside me like a thorn.

But how could I tell her about what I'd done to Domingo? And what he'd done to me in return? It wouldn't help things. It wouldn't make them better.

And she wouldn't look at me with compassion any longer, but horror.

Because the other thing she'd always given me was hope. Hope that one day I could be the man she saw when she looked at me. Hope that I could leave Domingo behind in the past for ever. And he wouldn't be if I told her what I'd done.

He'd be between us always.

So, no truth. But I couldn't keep shutting her out and locking myself away. That wasn't fair on her. That was about my own baggage, not hers, and she shouldn't have to bear the brunt. Besides, I wanted to be with her. I wanted to spend time with her. I didn't care what we did, just being together would be enough.

'I'm not going to the cottage today.' I brushed my finger over her cheek once again. 'I will spend it with you. That is, if you'd like that?'

Her smile was like dawn breaking over a delicate landscape, illuminating everything. Illuminating me. 'Oh, yes, I'd love that. What would you like to do?'

Warmth glowed inside me, as if the light in her face had somehow transferred itself into me. 'Well,' I said, 'I'm not sure. I've never done things with a friend before, so I was hoping you could tell me.'

'Idiot.' Her voice was full of affection. 'Of course you've done things with a friend before. We looked after a nest of sparrows together, remember?'

I raised an eyebrow. 'Jenny, I'm sorry, but I'm not looking after birds with you today. Or tomorrow. Or possibly ever again.'

She laughed, as if the sunshine had turned into sound. 'Good. Because I have other plans.'

CHAPTER SEVENTEEN

Jenny

IT SOON BECAME very clear to me that Con had put sex at the top of his list of things to do with friends, and he was puzzled when I suggested that we didn't have to spend all day in bed.

'But what else should we do?' he asked, and I could see that he genuinely didn't know.

Luckily for him, I did.

The thought of him being around all day, doing the kinds of things friends did with each other, filled me with happiness. Yes, I'd always been his friend, but that had been limited to the mansion in Madrid. We'd spent time with each other, but only in his study. Then I'd always wondered why he was so different with other people, but now I knew. It had been because of his father.

Today, though, Domingo was dead and Con wanted to spend time with me. I didn't want to think about the past. I didn't want to think about the future either. I wanted to enjoy the present while I could, because I had a sense that we had some difficult conversations ahead of us, about marriage and living arrangements and raising our child.

I'd voiced my worries about that, about my yearning for the kind of security and stability I'd never had growing up. Plus the doubt that underlaid all of that, which was the fear that he'd regret marrying me and leave me, the way my father had with my mother.

Some part of me knew he wasn't that kind of man and never had been, but I'd needed to hear his reassurance all the same. Except it hadn't completely eased all doubt. Some was still there, like a shard of ice in my heart.

He didn't love me, and he'd said he'd never be able to give me that, and somehow that made everything feel precarious.

But I wasn't going to think about it. And while spending time with him was probably a bad idea for my poor heart, I decided to ignore the danger. The future could take care of itself. I just wanted one day with the man I loved.

The weather was beautiful, so after we'd got out of bed—or rather when Con finally let me escape—and we'd had breakfast, I went off to speak with Mrs Mackenzie. Together we organised a picnic basket full of all Con's favourite foods—I was thrilled to find some chocolate-covered strawberries lurking in the fridge, since he did like chocolate—and some of mine, plus a bottle of champagne for him and some sparkling grape juice for me. Then I asked her where the best picnicking places were around the loch, and she patted my hand

and told me she'd get someone to arrange the picnic for us, so we didn't have to lug a heavy basket around.

When I told Con I'd organised a picnic, he made a show of being miffed that he hadn't arranged it himself, but I could tell he was secretly delighted. Which in turn delighted me.

Then he went and changed into some casual clothes—worn jeans and a black T-shirt—and every thought went out of my head.

I'd never seen him wear anything but handmade suits and formal wear, and he was to die for in those. In jeans and a T-shirt he was quite simply devastating. The cotton of his tee clung lovingly to his wide shoulders and broad chest, and the denim of his jeans hugged his powerful thighs. It almost made me consider scrapping the picnic and spending the rest of the day in bed, the way he'd suggested.

I'd looked around in the drawers for something casual to wear for myself, but found nothing. Apparently he hadn't thought I'd want to go traipsing around the loch. I didn't mind, though. Especially when he told me he'd prefer me to wear another wrap dress, since they were much easier to take off.

There was a trail around the loch, and at first he set a blistering pace, prompting me to grab his hand to slow him down. I told him that the whole point of this walk was to look at the scenery and talk to each other. He seemed mystified by that too, but he didn't let go of my hand, his fingers entwined with mine warm and strong.

The setting was beautiful, the deep valley and the

loch, the heather blooming on the slopes turning the whole valley purple.

'What made you buy this place?' I asked as we walked. 'It's a long way from Madrid.'

He gave me an enigmatic glance. 'That's exactly why. Because it's a long way from Madrid. There's no cell phone service either, which makes it the perfect place to retreat to.'

'From Domingo?'

'*Sí.*' He looked away from me, out over the loch. 'In the past when I came here I would dismiss all my staff for a week or so. Live in the house completely alone.' His mouth twisted wryly. 'Well, apart from Mrs Mackenzie.'

'Oh, you let her stay?'

He glanced back at me, wry amusement clear in his gaze too. 'I didn't "let" her do anything. She refused to leave. Said I needed someone to look after me.'

I grinned, charmed at the thought of Mrs Mackenzie bullying one of the most feared businessmen in Europe into being looked after. 'She's difficult to say no to, it's true.'

'Stubborn women plague my life.'

'Poor you.' I squeezed his hand, then after a moment asked, 'Why did you stay in Madrid? Why didn't you ever leave and go somewhere else?'

Something furious glittered briefly in his eyes. 'What? Run away like Valentin? No. I couldn't leave. Silver Inc is one of Europe's largest companies, and that made Domingo powerful. His influence spread everywhere, affecting many other companies and many other people. And no one knew what he was really like except me, so I had to stay to mitigate the damage he could do, to manage him.'

'Did that person have to be you?'

'He listened to me. I'd spent years turning myself into a carbon copy of him and, while I don't believe he was capable of trusting anyone, he certainly gave more weight to my opinions that anyone else's. I was able to guide him on certain policy changes.'

That didn't surprise me, not considering Con's deep protective streak. But I could also see that he was very angry with Valentin, and I wanted to know why. Obviously pretending you were dead for fifteen years wasn't going to endear you to anyone, and I could understand why Con was upset with him for that. But...there was more. Even when Con had spoken about Valentin rescuing his toy soldier he'd been furious. He'd said that Valentin had made things worse, and I could see that too, but... I was curious. I wanted to know more.

I wanted to know everything.

Still, there was a time and a place, and while I knew I could push him if I wanted to, I didn't want to right now. This was supposed to be a nice day for the two of us, so I squeezed his hand and changed the subject.

We talked about other things, such as how he preferred riding to hiking, and that there were stables here if I wanted to ride too. I'd never ridden a horse before, and of course he insisted that I needed to learn and that he would teach me himself. Then he went off into a long description of the whisky distillery he'd had built on the other side of the loch, an interest he'd been pursuing for a few years, and how their first single malt was due to be released soon.

It was clear from the gleam in his eyes that this was something he was passionate about, and I loved listening to him talk about it. That passion coloured his voice, softened the hard planes and angles of his face, making him even more ridiculously beautiful than he already was.

The picnic place Mrs Mackenzie had recommended was half an hour from the manor—a lovely flat area just across from the pebbly beach of the loch. A thick rug had been spread out over the heather, and all the picnic things laid out. There was no sign of paper plates or plastic cutlery and plastic glasses. Instead, the plates were porcelain, the cutlery silver, and the glasses cut crystal.

I watched Con's face as he examined the picnic and saw him smile. And when he looked at me his dark eyes were full of intensity. 'This is wonderful, Jenny. Thank you.'

He meant it, and that made me glow with pleasure.

I tugged on his hand to lead him to the rug. 'Come on. Let's have something to eat.'

He sat down and I insisted on serving him, putting on his plate all the delicacies I knew he liked—including the strawberries—then handing him a glass of champagne that was already opened and sitting in an ice bucket for us.

I loved doing things for him. I loved looking after him.

A peaceful silence reigned as we ate, and then, when

Con finally put down his plate, he said, 'These are all my favourite foods. How did you know what I liked?'

'I paid attention to you,' I said, pleased that he'd noticed. 'And I remembered what you like.' I paused, then added, 'I always liked taking care of you, too.'

The expression in his eyes shifted. 'Why did you sometimes take Domingo's hand? Those times he came into my study, when I'd tell you to leave and you wouldn't. You started talking to him instead.'

I shrugged. 'Domingo didn't like me. I made him uncomfortable. I'm not sure why. When I tried to talk to him he'd ignore me and just…leave. So when I noticed that you didn't seem to like his visits, I did it more.'

The look on Con's face was impenetrable. 'You were protecting me?'

I had my legs tucked under me, my plate at my side, sipping on my grape juice—which was delightfully dry and not at all as sweet as I'd dreaded.

I blushed. 'I know, it's stupid. It's not like I'm tall or powerful or anything, but… Well, I tried.'

His eyes were as black as space and they watched me keenly, though I couldn't tell what he was thinking.

'Domingo had an estate in the Caribbean that he used to take Valentin and I to,' he said after a moment. 'Valentin got to know a girl from a neighbouring estate and she became his friend. He used to meet her on a secret beach, very much against our father's wishes.'

I wasn't sure why he was telling me this, but there was no way I was going to interrupt him so I stayed silent, watching him.

'That girl was Olivia,' he went on. 'Her family used to holiday on the same island.'

A shock of surprise went through me. 'Really?'

'Yes. I was…jealous. Not of Valentin, but of her. She took away the one person I had, because he didn't want to spend any time with me when she was there, he only wanted to spend time with her. I was angry with him for choosing her over me. And he always made our situation worse by not doing what Domingo said and making him angry. I felt that Domingo even liked it when Valentin rebelled, and that somehow he preferred Valentin's rebellions to me doing everything he said.' Con paused, looking down at the champagne in his hand. 'He preferred resistance. He liked it… Anyway, I was furious that Valentin was disobeying Domingo by continuing to see Olivia, by developing a friendship we weren't allowed and by preferring to spend time with her than with me. So, I…went to Domingo and told him what Valentin was doing.'

A thread of tension wound through me.

'Papa was furious. He ordered Valentin to stop seeing her, but Valentin wouldn't. So Domingo locked him in his room. He wasn't allowed to come out until he agreed to stop seeing Olivia. But Valentin refused.' Con's perfect face was hard, his mouth a grim line. 'I pleaded with him to agree, because I knew Domingo. He'd keep Valentin in that room for ever if he had to. But Valentin kept saying no. He stayed in that room for six months.'

Ice pooled in my gut. Six months? He'd stayed in his room for six months?

'He wouldn't listen to me,' Con went on, his accent deepening. 'He refused. I needed him, but his battle with Domingo was more important than I was. Even protecting Olivia wasn't as important. I didn't understand him—I never did. And in the end all I could do was find the key and give it to him, because I knew he'd never give in. And I was the one who'd put him there.' Con looked at me, his gaze sharp enough to cut. 'You wanted to know why I kicked down your door? Because I spent hours, days, sitting outside Val's locked door, desperate for him to come out. And he never did.'

There was anguish in his eyes, and grief.

'Con—' I began.

'No, I haven't finished.' His voice was hoarse. 'I'm telling you this because you asked me a few days ago who protected me, and the answer is that you did. You protected me, Jenny. And you will never know how much that meant to me. But you have to understand that you also need protection. I always thought the danger came from my father, but it doesn't, not any more.' He took a breath, then caught my gaze. 'It comes from me.'

I blinked at him, not understanding. 'What do you mean, the danger comes from you?'

'Emotions are grenades. They can explode at any time. You saw what happened when you locked the door on me. And when Valentin refused to give Olivia up. When he left me—' Con stopped, darkness in his eyes. 'I am that grenade, Jenny. I am unstable when I let my emotions get the better of me. And when that happens, you are at risk.' He took another breath. 'I want to be your friend. I don't want to cause you any more pain than I already have. But when we get back to London you will have to allow me to keep some emotional distance from you.'

I stared at him in shock, trying to process what he'd said. 'I don't understand. You're not unstable. You're not a danger. What on earth makes you think that?'

He glanced down at the heather in bloom all around us. 'Kicking down your door. Getting Val locked in his room. Being so angry with him. There have been other instances.'

'Con—'

'No, please.' He glanced up again. 'Not now. Let's have this day just for us.'

I wanted to push. I wanted to tell him he was wrong, that he wasn't unstable or volatile or a grenade. He was only a man who felt deeply and who'd never learned how to deal with his emotions. Who'd been scarred by his childhood. That was all. He wasn't a danger, not to me.

But he was right. This day was for us, not for the past, so I put down my grape juice, then went over to him and relieved him of his glass. Then I wriggled into his lap, winding my arms around him. I didn't speak. I simply pressed my face to his throat, holding him tightly.

He was still a moment, his big, powerful body tense. Then his arms closed around me and he crushed me to him, burying his face in my hair.

We stayed like that for a long time, and then Con released me. But only so he could pull me down on the picnic blanket beside him. Then he tugged open the tie of my dress and spread the fabric out, baring me to the deep blue sky above. He bent his head and kissed me, his mouth tasting of champagne and the delicious dark flavour that was all him. Then he got rid of my clothes and turned his hunger on me, making a meal of my body, feasting on me as if he'd never had anything quite so delicious.

Only when he had me quivering in delight and shaking with need did he strip his own clothes off and rise above me, naked and magnificent, his olive skin burnished by the sun. Then he thrust into me in one hard movement, making me cry out his name.

And when he moved, deep and slow, turning my pleasure into white-hot passion in seconds flat, I cried out his name again.

Perhaps it was then that I knew, even though consciously I didn't want to admit it. Knew that no matter how many months had passed, and no matter how many promises I'd made to myself, no matter how many stern talking-tos I'd given myself, I was still in love with him.

And friendship would never be enough.

CHAPTER EIGHTEEN

Constantine

I FORGOT ABOUT going to the cottage. I forgot about the company. I even forgot about Valentin. All I wanted to do was spend time with Jenny.

I taught her the basics of riding, making sure to put her on the gentlest horse, and took her for a walk around one of the fields. She turned out to be a natural on horseback, which thrilled her since, as she told me, she hadn't been a natural at anything before.

Another day I took her on the tour of my distillery. The business of whisky-making took time and care, and I'd found it the perfect escape from the day-to-day running of Silver Inc. It had also helped that it had nothing whatsoever to do with Domingo.

It mattered to me more than I'd thought that she was interested in it, and asked all kinds of questions on the tour. I'd wanted to give her a taste of our first batch, but obviously that would have to wait until after the baby was born.

She was so easy to be with. Easy to share with. She

made every day brighter, and I'd forgotten how simply being around her brought me joy.

Except it made the beast in me hungrier and hungrier. As if all the time in the world with her wouldn't be enough. Nothing would. I wanted to keep her here in Glen Creag, never let her leave. We could bring our child up here and it would be perfect. I could have them both all to myself for ever.

But that was what the beast wanted, not the man, and I would never give in to it. No matter what Papa had said to me that night, I wasn't just like him. I was different, I was better, and even though it was getting harder and harder to be better where Jenny was concerned, I had to be for her sake.

When we finally left Glen Creag I would have to be ruthless with myself. I'd warned her that I would have to retain a certain amount of emotional distance but, since I wasn't willing to hurt her, I couldn't completely withdraw my friendship from her, not again.

It would be difficult—torture—but I could do it.

I also had to be strong with regard to my other little secret.

Since that day of the wonderful little picnic she'd arranged for me, when I'd nearly told her about it, I'd managed to keep it locked down.

She had to keep believing I was a good man, keep thinking that I would make a good father. Because if she didn't I would be lost. I would have nothing to aim for, nothing to strive for. I wanted to be the man she saw when she looked at me, both for her and for our child, which meant I could never tell her.

Which was fine. She might get under most of my defences with pathetic ease, but not that one. That one would have to remain obdurate.

A few days after I'd taken her on a tour of the distillery, and after another riding trip, where this time I brought a picnic for her, I decided that there was one last place on the estate that I wanted her to see.

My collection room.

I hoped that sharing it with her would make her feel at ease. I'd caught her looking speculatively at me a couple of times, and wondered if it was to do with my slip at the picnic, but she hadn't broached the topic again. Perhaps if I gave her this last piece of myself she'd forget about the thing I didn't want to tell her.

I found her curled up in one of the armchairs in the small library a few days later, with her nose in a book. It reminded me very much of how she'd used to be in my study, tucked away in the armchair, reading. She'd look up from her book and see me, and then she'd smile, and her face would light up.

My chest tightened as she did that now, putting down her book and looking up at me, her smile lighting the room in the same way it always did.

'What are we going to do today? Please tell me we're going riding.'

I smiled at her eagerness. 'This afternoon, perhaps. Right now, though, I have something I want to show you.' I held out my hand.

Instantly she got up and came over to me, her fingers threading through mine. 'Oh, what?'

Her hand felt small and delicate and warm, so I held it gently. 'You'll see.'

I let her out of the room and headed towards the front door.

'You know, Con,' she murmured as we stepped outside, 'we've skirted around it, but we need to talk about a few things.'

We did. Our wedding loomed, and so did the question of where we would live and other such practicalities. I needed to deal with the Valentin situation also. But I didn't want to think about those things right now. They could wait.

'We will,' I said. 'Later.'

I led her across the grass towards the cottage and she didn't speak, although her fingers tightened around mine.

Inside the cottage, I went to the shelving unit and pressed the hidden button to reveal the palm lock. I unlocked the door, pulled it open, and gestured for her to go in first.

She gave me a worried look, her beautiful brown eyes questioning. 'Are you sure?'

'Yes.'

'Okay.' She went to the doorway and stepped through it into the room beyond.

I'd thought I'd feel tense at her presence there, the way I had before, but I didn't. As soon as she stepped through the doorway something clicked into place. A sense of rightness. As if she belonged there, along with all of my other precious items.

I followed behind her, watching as she stared around

at the glass cases and shelves of my collection. At the things that were precious and the things that were not. Things worth millions and things worth nothing at all.

'What…is this?' Her voice was quiet as she stared around, her eyes wide.

'You know I told you that I wasn't allowed anything as a child? No toys. No friends. No pets. Only school materials and the clothes on our backs. We weren't even allowed books to read. So when I was finally old enough to be out from under Domingo's thumb, I decided I would collect things that I liked.'

She paused beside a case that contained coins. I had some old Spanish doubloons, a few from Ancient Roman, one or two Greek. I even had a *daric*, a gold coin from ancient Persia.

'Why didn't you want me to come in that day I found you in here?' she murmured, gazing at the coins. 'You were furious with me. I know you were.'

'Because this collection is private, and some of these things are very personal to me. I suppose hiding them is a habit I've got into. With Domingo, you couldn't let him see that anything was important to you, because he'd take it away. So I found it easier to keep everything hidden.'

Perhaps I hadn't needed to in the past few years, but by then it had become a habit too hard to break.

Jenny moved on to my small collection of mechanical toys, mostly from the Victorian era, staring at them in wonder. 'I can understand that. You have so many different things…'

'I collect anything that takes my fancy.'

She examined the collection of swords and knives from different parts of the world—some historic, some modern—that I'd had mounted on the wall. Then went on to another case full of gems, crystals and geodes. A few were very valuable, while some weren't. Some were just ones I liked.

She paused, staring at them, and her mouth curved. 'You have a rock collection, Con.'

I loved it when she teased me. There was so much affection in her tone.

I raised a brow, mock-stern. 'Yes. What of it?'

She grinned. 'And coins and swords and toys and—' Abruptly, she broke off, her expression changing, her smile fading away, leaving her looking almost stricken. Her dark eyes seemed liquid in the light of the room.

Tension gripped me. 'Jenny? What is it?'

She turned away, moving over to one of the other shelves before pausing again. I knew what she was looking at. My toy soldier.

She didn't say anything, staring down at the piece of plastic sitting on the shelf.

I went over to where she stood, coming up beside her. 'What's wrong?'

'That's your toy,' she said quietly, ignoring my question. 'That's your toy soldier, isn't it? The one Valentin threw onto the roof.'

'Yes.' I wasn't sure where she was going with this.

'And all of this…' She turned, looking up me, tears in her eyes. 'Rocks and coins and swords… You missed out on so much.' Her voice went hoarse. 'And you were hurt so badly. I can't...'

A tear slid down her cheek, making my chest feel so tight I could hardly breathe.

Reaching out, I pulled her into my arms and gathered her close. 'I didn't bring you here to upset you.' I pressed a kiss to the top of her head. 'I only wanted to share it with you. Something important to me.'

'I know.' The words were muffled against my shirt. 'And I'm honoured, Con. But it makes me so sad to think about the little boy you were and what you never got to have.'

'That's all in the past now,' I said gruffly.

She looked up, her face flushing pink with emotion. 'I don't want this for our child. I don't want him or her to miss out on a single thing or to feel as if they're not loved. Not even a little bit. We can't let that happen. We can't. Promise me.'

The tension gripped tighter. 'I can promise you that they won't miss out on anything.'

Her gaze flickered and she bit her lip. 'You said that love isn't something you can give. Do you still mean that?'

A blade slid between my ribs, so sharp I barely felt it go in. Yet it was there, deep in my gut, radiating pain. But ever since I'd met her I'd spent my life protecting her, and I wasn't going to stop now. Especially not now we were expecting a child.

She must have read my expression, because the look in her eyes changed. 'Oh, Con, please don't say—'

I let her go abruptly and took a step back. I hadn't

wanted to hurt her—not again—but this was unavoidable. 'Yes,' I said. 'Yes, I still mean it.'

Anguish flickered over her face. 'Why? I don't understand.'

'Because love isn't something I can—'

'No,' she interrupted, her voice quivering. *'No.'* The anguish disappeared, leaving fury hot and bright in her eyes. 'Don't tell me you can't, or that you're not able to. Don't lie to me, Constantine.'

'Jenny—'

'No,' she said again, her hands in fists at her sides. 'There's something you're not telling me, something you're hiding. I think you almost let it slip at our picnic, but you didn't want to talk about it.' She took a step towards me. 'What is it? It's something to do with these lies you believe about love, isn't it?'

You have to tell her. You can't hide it.

Ice sat in my gut, hard and jagged and sharp. I hadn't wanted to tell her. I hadn't *ever* wanted to tell her. But there was no escaping it now. I could have given her some ridiculous excuse, some meaningless justification, but I couldn't do that to her, not when it concerned our child. She deserved better than that.

I had to tell her the truth. Even if it changed things. Even if it meant putting her and our baby beyond my reach for ever. And maybe it would even be better this way. Better a short, sharp pain now, so that she could heal, rather than a prolonged agony, especially an agony that might have the potential to affect our son or daughter.

'You're right,' I said, ignoring the pain that lay deep

in my heart. 'There is something I'm not telling you. I didn't ever want to tell you. I wanted to keep you and the baby safe. But… You deserve to know. It's not fair to keep you in the dark.'

Her face had gone white. 'What is it?'

'The night Valentin escaped his room I knew he was gone for good. That he wouldn't ever return. He had… left me.'

I could still feel the rage. It was still there. Rage at Valentin, rage at myself, rage at my father.

'It was my fault. If I hadn't told Domingo about him and Olivia then none of it would have happened. I was…furious. At myself, at Val, at Papa. I went to Papa's study and I stormed inside. I hadn't ever rebelled against him, not like Val. I did everything he said usually. But…not that night.'

Even to my own ears my voice sounded harsh, metallic.

'He was sitting in a chair, reading a book, and I lost my temper. I was tall at seventeen, and I was strong, and so when I pulled him out of his chair he came easily. I'd surprised him.'

Jenny's eyes darkened, but she didn't look away and she didn't speak.

'I don't remember much of what happened then, just an explosion of rage and the feel of my fist connecting with his face. The next thing I was aware of was him on the floor, his face a bloody mess.'

Every part of my body was tight, the pain radiating outward, but I forced it away. Turned myself cold, hard. Impervious.

'My fists were bloody too, my knuckles raw, and he…he was laughing. He was laughing at me.'

My jaw ached, everything ached.

'And do you know what he said, Jenny? He said "Finally. I was beginning to think you had none of my blood. But you do, boy. Deep down, you're just like me."'

Jenny blinked, a small crease between her silky brows. 'But…you're not, Con.' She said it as if it was self-evident. 'You're nothing like him.'

Of course she would say that. She liked to see the best in people, and that was one of the wonderful things about her. But that meant she minimised the worst. Especially the worst that could do harm.

'Aren't I?' I stayed very still, so I wouldn't give in to the need to pull her into my arms and hold her, never let her go. 'I thought I was. That night I decided never to lose myself to anger again, never to lose myself to *any* emotion again. And for years I managed to do that. To not be the man *he* saw. Until you came along. When you were a child it was easy to distance myself, but… not when you grew up.'

'Con—'

'That night in the garden I lost all control,' I went on, over the top of her, because I had to get this out, she had to know. 'I hurt you. I got you pregnant. Then I kidnapped you and stole you away to come here. I kicked down your door, laid my hands on you. I…' I stopped, breathing hard, feeling as if all the air in the room had been sucked away. 'You bring out all these feelings in me, feelings I cannot control. And it's dangerous. Don't you understand? It's dangerous.'

She stared at me, so pale and lovely, her eyes dark. 'No, actually, I *don't* understand. You've never made me feel afraid, not ever. You're not dangerous and neither are your emotions. You just…feel deeply. Besides, everything you do is about protecting other people, about protecting me.'

I shook my head, my heart beating too fast. Because it was clear that she didn't understand. 'I'm not dangerous now because I remain in control of myself. But I have no control around you. And the more time I spend with you, the more I want. And I can't want. I can't feel so hungry, so desperate. Because I would never forgive myself if I hurt you, and I'd rather die than hurt our child.'

She took a step towards me, her hand outstretched, but something in my gaze must have stopped her, because she lowered it all of a sudden. 'You wouldn't, though. I know you wouldn't. Those birds that you looked after—'

'A child is not a nest of birds,' I ground out. 'And I didn't feel anything for those birds.'

'But you feel something for me, don't you? And for our baby?'

I didn't say anything. I didn't have to.

'Oh, Con,' she murmured, her voice hoarse. 'Why didn't you tell me this?'

'I didn't want you to know. I didn't want you to see…' I gritted my teeth. 'I didn't want you to see Domingo when you looked at me.'

'And I don't.' She closed the distance between us, so small, yet indomitable. 'I never have. Do you know what I see when I look at you, Constantine Silvera? I see the man I've loved for as long as I can remember.'

I could see that love in her eyes. It shone so bright. She didn't hide it. She didn't control it. It radiated from her like heat from the sun.

That love was her light, and I couldn't dim it. I couldn't bear to be the one who made it go dark. And I would. At some point in time, I would.

I was too much like my father and I knew it. I'd always known it.

The pain inside me turned to agony, but I crushed it. Pain had been a constant in my life anyway. It was nothing new.

'I'm sorry,' I said, my voice frozen all the way through. 'I cannot risk it. I cannot risk you.'

'What does that mean?'

The pain had gone now. There was only the ice settling around my heart and it was a relief, so I let it. It was the only way I could survive the decision I had to make, and I knew it.

'It means you have to leave. Go back to London. Go back to your life. I will arrange a flight for you. You can be home by tomorrow night.'

She was staring at me now as if I was a total stranger. 'Go home? But for how long? What about the wedding?'

'How long? For ever, Jenny,' I said gently. 'Because there will be no wedding. I cannot marry you.'

CHAPTER NINETEEN

Jenny

I STARED INTO Con's beautiful hard face, looking for some sign that he didn't mean what he'd said, even that this was some elaborate joke. But it was clear that he did mean it. He meant every word.

Pain collected inside me, tears in my eyes already from the evidence of a destroyed boyhood all around us in the rocks and coins and weapons and toys. A collection of things a little boy would have loved. A little boy who'd have kept them in a shoebox under his bed or in his closet. His favourite rocks and a coin or two. A wooden sword and a mechanical toy. A plastic soldier…

A combination of rare and common, priceless and worthless, and all kept behind a locked door in a vault, as if they were the most precious things on the earth. It broke my heart.

Con broke my heart.

He had lost so much, and although he was the successful CEO of one of Europe's biggest companies, at heart he was still a lonely little boy. A little boy who surrounded himself with things because it was easier to love a thing than a person.

I ached for that boy. Because I knew him. That boy was like me. The kid who felt everything so deeply, whose emotions were big and painful and raw. Who cared so much and who wanted more than anything on earth to love and to be loved in return.

That boy thought his emotions were dangerous, thought *he* was dangerous.

He wasn't, though, I knew that. All his life he'd been protecting people, protecting me, and he hadn't done that because he didn't care.

He cared too much, that was his problem. And he didn't know how to handle it.

But I did. I could help him. I could show him how.

I ignored what he'd said about me leaving and him not marrying me, and said, 'So you'd believe your psychopathic father over me?' I didn't try to hide the growing anger in my voice. 'Is that what you're saying? He told you that you were like him and so you believe him.'

Con's obsidian gaze glittered, sharp and unyielding. 'You think it was just what he said? I have always battled to stay in control—'

'Because you were never taught how to deal with your emotions!' I interrupted, suddenly furious. Not at him, but at the father who'd scarred him and the brother who'd left him. 'You were brought up by a psychopath, Con. No wonder you think all your feelings are toxic.'

'I can't put you at risk.' There was iron in his voice. 'I have done nothing but make your life miserable for years and I will not do it any longer. Especially now we have a child to consider.'

I felt as if there was stone stuck in my throat, making it hard to breathe, to swallow, and what I wanted was to throw myself into his arms. Tell him it was okay, that we could talk about this later, just let us have another few days of happiness.

But I couldn't do it. I couldn't give in. If I wanted to have him—if I wanted to have any kind of relationship with him at all—I couldn't let him pull away from me.

If he wasn't going to fight for us, then I would.

'I'm sure that sounds great in your head,' I said, steel to his iron. 'I'm sure that all sounds very noble. But it's just an excuse, isn't it? It's just an excuse so you don't have to deal with difficult things.'

Black fire flared in his eyes. 'You think I haven't had to deal with difficulties? You really think you can say that to me?'

But I wasn't having that. I wasn't going to have him walk all over me, tell me I was wrong, break my heart, because he thought he was protecting me. He wasn't protecting me. He was protecting himself. And if I wanted him it wasn't just him I'd have to fight, but Domingo too.

'I can say whatever I like to you,' I said fiercely. 'Because I love you and I want you. I want to spend the rest of my life with you. I want us to be a family and I think you want that too. I know you do. You're desperate for it, just like me.' I stared at him, letting him see the depth of what I felt for him, see my love for him in all its painful, ecstatic glory. 'But you're still letting your father make your decisions for you, Con. And you're still believing his lies. And if you can't see that, it's because you don't want to.'

Anger flashed in his gaze, and a deep pain.

Suddenly he was in front of me, his warm hands cupping my face with such gentleness I nearly wept. Even in a fury he was gentle.

'I can't,' he said, as if the words had been ripped from him. 'I can't take the risk. You and our baby… you're precious. I can't… I don't…'

'You can take the risk. You can. And if you can't trust yourself, then trust me. Trust my love for you. When have I ever let you down?'

His gaze searched mine and I could see the desperation in it. I wanted to tell him that it was okay, that he could let go, that his love wasn't something to be afraid of, but something to celebrate. But I saw the moment when he made the decision not to make that leap, to step back from the edge. To trust in the lies of a psychopath rather than me.

And wasn't that the story of my life? I hadn't been enough for my father, who'd left, or my mother, who'd gone searching for something she'd never been able to get from me. Why would it be any different with Con?

My heart broke then, into tiny, jagged pieces. Because as much as I wanted to push him further, I didn't have the will for it. His whole life had been a battle, so why make this just another fight? He wasn't going to change his mind. He'd decided. And there was nothing I could say that could convince him.

He thought he was doing this to protect me and our

child, so why not let him believe that? Why not let him have that peace of mind?

It hurt. It hurt so much. But this wasn't about me, and I didn't want it to be.

It was only and had only ever been about him.

It was only a broken heart. Nothing major.

'Okay,' I said croakily. 'If that's what you feel you need to do.'

I'd sworn I'd never cry in front of him again, and yet more and more tears were gathering in my eyes, and no matter how hard I tried I couldn't blink them away.

A muscle ticked in his jaw, but he was already retreating from me, ice in his gaze. Ice right the way through his soul. 'Don't cry, Jenny.' He let me go and stepped back. 'It's better this way.'

I could have turned around and walked away right then. I could have given in to anger and kept everything inside, met him ice for ice and not allowed him a thing.

But I didn't want that for him. What I wanted was to give him one last thing to carry, a piece of myself he could take with him wherever he went. So he'd know that at least there was one person in this world who cared about him.

I lifted my chin and let the tears fall, because those tears were for him and what did it matter that he could see them? What did it matter that this was agony? This agony was love, and I couldn't keep it inside me any longer.

'I love you,' I said clearly. 'I love you so much, Constantine Silvera. I always have and I always will, and there is nothing you can do to change it. Nothing you can do that will make me love you any less.'

His expression shifted then, a crack in his icy detached mask giving me a glimpse of something molten and raging beneath it. 'Jenny, I—'

'No,' I interrupted. 'No. I haven't finished. I'm telling you this because I want you to know. I want you to be absolutely certain. If you think you're alone in this world, you are not. There will be two people in it—' I touched my stomach so he'd know who else I meant '—who love you utterly and without reservation.'

That raging volcanic thing in his eyes burned bright for one shining moment. Then he glanced away briefly, and when he looked back it was gone. Ice-cold Constantine Silvera was in charge again.

'Please do not worry about money,' he said, as if I hadn't spoken. 'You and the baby will be financially secure. I'll see to it. And I'll also see to it that you will be well protected.'

The tears slid down my cheeks. 'You probably won't want to hear this either, but I'm going to say it anyway. You deserve to be loved. And you deserve to love in return.'

His face remained expressionless. 'Maybe,' he said blankly. 'Maybe not.'

That night in the garden, where I'd felt so destroyed, so broken, I felt those same things now. Yet I could also feel a determination inside me, a steel that perhaps had always been there. A steel that came from love. Love for my child, and love for the man in front of me, and last but not least, it came from hope.

Hope that one day he'd find his way out of the darkness.

Hope that one day he'd come back to us.

I closed the distance between us, going up to him and lifting a hand, wanting to touch him one last time. I brushed my fingers along his hard jaw, feeling the warmth of his skin that was the truth of him, not the black ice in his eyes.

He said nothing, his big, powerful body tense as a wound spring.

'I'll go, but know that I'm not leaving you,' I said softly. 'I will never leave you, not in spirit. I'll be there whenever you need me, Con, and so will our child.'

I wasn't going to change his mind. If he was going to come to me he'd have to make that decision himself. I couldn't make it for him.

I let my hand drop away from his face and moved past him to the door, stepping out into the office. Then I went out across the grass to the manor.

I didn't do anything about the tears that poured down my cheeks.

I let them fall.

CHAPTER TWENTY

Constantine

THAT NIGHT, AFTER THE helicopter had come to take Jenny back to Edinburgh had gone, and there was nothing left for me but the echoing corridors of the manor and the last, elusive threads of her scent hanging in the air, I went out to the cottage and called Valentin.

I'd been putting it off for too long. He had to be dealt with.

Unfortunately, the conversation was not a productive one. I was angry, and in pain, and I allowed my temper to get the better of me. Another reason that it was better that Jenny wasn't here.

Every relationship I had, I seemed to break.

I tried to bury my emotions with work, mobilising my legal team to fight Valentin's claim. Then I went about making sure that Jenny and our child were taken care of.

I didn't think too deeply about her, didn't think about that phone call with Valentin either. Neither of those things would touch me. Neither of those were going to matter.

Instead, I found the detachment that had kept me going for fifteen years and held on to it as tightly as I could.

Three days passed with aching slowness.

I stayed in the cottage. I couldn't bring myself to be in the manor, where Jenny's scent still lingered. Where everywhere I looked I could see her. Curled up in an armchair. Sitting on a dining chair telling me about some book she'd been reading as she ate ice cream. Squealing on the pebbly beach of the loch as she tested the icy water with small bare toes. Lying naked in my bed and lifting her arms to me, welcoming me into her warmth and her softness. Her understanding and her compassion.

I ached and nothing could ease it. All I could do was distract myself from my empty house, and my empty bed, and the emptiness in my heart that ached and ached right down to my bones.

In the end I spent a lot of time in my collection room, adjusting the displays and unpacking new items. Normally I got tremendous satisfaction out of those small tasks, and yet as I flicked open a box containing an emerald I felt…nothing.

I put the box down on a shelf and looked around at my collection with growing disquiet. These things were all mine, and yet now they all seemed…ridiculous.

What had Jenny said? *'Rocks and coins and swords… You missed out on so much.'*

I had missed out. I had missed out on everything.

And now I was trying to fill that emptiness inside me with things. With a little boy's pathetic collection of rocks and coins and toys. A leftover from the childhood he'd never managed to leave behind.

'You're still letting your father make your decisions for you, Con. And you're still believing his lies. And if you can't see that, it's because you don't want to.'

I took a shaken breath, her words before she'd left echoing in my head as I stared around at the remnants of my childhood. Seeing them finally with new eyes.

This wasn't a collection of things I'd always wanted and never had.

These were reminders of what Domingo had done to me. Reminders of Domingo's hold on me. Things I was clinging to, to fill up that emptiness inside me. An emptiness that could never be filled. Not while Jenny wasn't here.

She was the only one who made me feel I wasn't the same kind of psychopath Domingo had been. The only one who made me feel I could be a good man. The only one who'd made me *want* to be a good man.

'So you believe your psychopathic father over me? He told you that you were like him and so you believe him?'

I paused beside the toy soldier sitting on its shelf. The soldier Domingo had tried to make me burn, and that Valentin had taken and thrown on the roof.

Why had I kept it? Why had I kept any of these things when they were reminders of all the ways Domingo had hurt me? And not just me, but Valentin too.

He had hurt us, twisted us, turned us into his image.

Val escaped, but you never did. You're still that lost boy with bloody knuckles, listening to a man you hated telling you that your worst fear is true.

She was right, my Jenny. She'd been right all along. He still had a hold on me, even all these years later, and I'd never be free of him until all these reminders were gone.

I picked up the soldier, the edges of the plastic cutting into me, then slowly and deliberately I crushed it.

Then I turned and systematically smashed every case in the room.

'Feel better?'

I stopped dead, surrounded by broken glass, my breath heaving, my hands bleeding from all the cuts I'd received.

That voice. It was familiar.

I turned.

Valentin stood in the doorway, leaning against the frame. The brother I'd last seen three weeks ago, striding into the ballroom to tell me he was going to relieve me of my company. Stealing my bride.

His posture was casual, but the look on his face— the same face I saw every day in the mirror—was not. His gaze burned.

I couldn't speak. I couldn't trust myself, not after our last conversation on the phone.

He gazed dispassionately around the room and then looked back at me. 'Are you done?'

He spoke in Spanish, our mother tongue, and he looked the same as he always had. He looked like my brother, my twin.

'What are you doing here? How did you—?'

'I came back to London with Olivia. We're married, by the way, and blissfully happy. You can congratulate me at any time.'

I stared at him, my knuckles stinging, shock resounding through me, unable to think of a single word to say.

'Fine, don't, then.' He shoved himself away from the door frame and took a couple of steps into the ruined room, not paying any attention to it. 'Jenny contacted me. I like her, by the way. She and Olivia got on like a house on fire.' He took another step, his footsteps crunching on the glass. 'She told me that you've hidden yourself away and are refusing all calls. That you're quite certain that it's safer for her and your baby to be far away from you. She's worried about you.' He took another step. 'So I thought I'd better come up here and check, to make sure you're okay.'

I'd thought about this moment, the moment when I'd see Val again. Thought about all the things I would say to him. Cutting things. Hurtful things. Furious things.

Yet seeing him, with the last remains of our twisted childhood lying in ruins around us, all my rage drained suddenly away.

'I'm sorry,' I said hoarsely. 'For the last conversation we had. I was angry. I've been angry at you for a long time. But all of that was my fault. Olivia…what Papa did to you…shutting you in your room… It was my fault.'

All the polished charm dropped from Val's face and his eyes darkened as he looked at me. 'No, Con. No.' There was anguish in his words. 'I'm to blame as much as you. I left you alone with him. I let you believe I was dead. And... *Dios*, you will never know how sorry I am for that.'

Such a simple thing to say, and yet it made the pain in my heart ease somehow.

'I had to go,' he went on, his voice getting rough. 'With Domingo it would never have ended—only with one of us dead.' He took a breath. 'That phone call... I am sorry for that too. I still had issues to work out as well.'

'So what changed?' I asked. 'Between now and three days ago?'

His mouth curved, his face softening, his eyes lighting up. 'Let's just say that being with Olivia changed me. Made me think about the past and realise a few things.' His gaze focused on me. 'You're right to be angry with me, Con.'

'No,' I said, straightening. 'No, I'm not. You were a victim as much as I was.' I looked down at my hands, at the blood on them, remembering another occasion where my hands had been bloody. 'I need to escape him somehow. But I... I don't know how to move past this.'

'I think you do. I think the way to move past this is in London, pregnant with your child.'

The words cut through me like a knife.

Valentin didn't look away. 'I know you,' he said quietly. 'We're twins, remember? Once something is ours, we never let it go and I don't think you want to let her go.'

I looked away, the beast in my heart desperate. 'How can I? There are things I haven't told you. Reasons she needs to be protected. No one can know that I—'

'No,' Val interrupted quietly. 'What she needs is to be loved.'

The words fell into the stillness like a stone in a quiet lake, creating ripples.

She *did* need to be loved. And I had loved her. No, I *still* loved her—deeply, madly, without reservation.

Except that wasn't right either. Because it *wasn't* without reservation. I was holding a piece of myself back.

The piece of myself I'd always thought was my father.

'Do you know what I see when I look at you, Constantine Silvera? I see the man I've loved for as long as I can remember.'

I'd told her what I'd done, what Domingo had said to me all those years ago, yet nothing had changed for her. She still loved me. She still saw the man I wanted to be for her. So why did I still believe him?

But I knew why. She had been right about that, too.

I was protecting myself. Distancing myself so I didn't have to face up to the fact I had no idea how to manage the emotions inside me. The deep, hot, possessive yearning for her. The beast I couldn't control.

I'd told myself I hadn't wanted to expose her to that, but the truth was I hadn't wanted to expose myself.

Vulnerable Jenny. Fragile Jenny. Soft Jenny.

Yet she was none of those things. Soft on the outside, but steel and strength down to her core.

It was me who was the fragile one.

Me who could break.

'I don't know if I can.' My voice was as cracked and jagged as shattered glass.

Valentin let out a soft breath. 'You can. Our father broke us, but that doesn't mean we have to stay broken. We can choose to heal.'

And suddenly all I could see was Jenny's lovely face. Jenny standing in front of me, her brown eyes full of warmth and compassion. Full of love. A complicated mixture of strength and vulnerability I hadn't thought possible.

She was vulnerable, yes, but strong. Fearful, yet full of courage.

Love had given her that. Love had made her vulnerable, but love had also given her bravery. Love had made her powerful.

I'd told her I could never give her love and yet she loved me, and she'd told me she always would. I might have sent her away, but she hadn't left. I could feel her still in my heart, a warm, glowing light that refused all my efforts to freeze it. That was starting to melt the icy edges of my soul.

Was it really that simple? Could I really make a choice? The choice to stay broken, as Val had said, because I was broken. Or choose Jenny. Choose our child. Choose love.

She was so strong, my Jenny. How could I be any less? And Val was right. She *should* be loved. She *needed* to be loved. She was always so concerned about everyone else's feelings. She never put herself first.

But she should. *Someone* should.

And that someone should be me.

She was in my heart, in my soul. She was part of me. And I loved her.

The warmth inside me glowed brighter, stronger, melting away the ice around my heart, cracking all my armour. And I couldn't bear it. I couldn't bear being without her one second longer.

I turned to the doorway and without a word headed straight for it.

'I take it you're going to London?' Val asked from behind me. 'I'll just clean up here, shall I?'

I didn't answer.

I left him to it.

CHAPTER TWENTY-ONE

Jenny

I HADN'T BROUGHT an umbrella, so I got soaked on my walk from the tube station to my flat. My dress was clinging uncomfortably to my skin as I put the key in the lock and opened the door, chilling me to the bone.

I was feeling very low. It had been a long day at the shelter, which always took it out of me. I often felt emotionally drained afterwards, and for the past few days I'd felt even worse.

I missed Con so badly. Every minute I'd think staying away wasn't worth it, and I'd nearly go to book myself a ticket to Edinburgh, only to remember that I wasn't doing this for me, that I couldn't go to him.

It was his decision to remain alone, not mine, and forcing myself on him would only make things more difficult.

I went into the kitchen and made myself a hot cup of tea, shivering in my damp dress and trying to fight the memories that always claimed me whenever I was alone. Memories of purple heather and Con's black eyes. Of the way they'd light up whenever he talked about something he was passionate about. Of the way his mouth would soften into an almost-smile when he was amused. Of the way he'd touched me, sometimes with such demand he'd set me on fire, and sometimes with such tenderness he'd made me cry.

Of that room full of things that were precious to him.

He was a man desperately in search of something to ease the loneliness inside him, just like my mother. And, just like her, he couldn't see that that something had been right in front of him all this time.

The flat was dark, and when I felt the baby give a little kick, tears started in my eyes. I put my hand on my stomach. 'It's okay, little one. We have to hope Daddy will change his mind one day. And he will. I'm sure of it.'

Except I wasn't at all sure he would.

A knock came on the door and I sighed, debating whether or not to answer it, since I wasn't up for visitors. But when the knock came again, and louder this time, I pulled a face and went into the hall to open it.

A man stood on the steps outside, rain soaking his expensive suit and catching in his eyelashes, turning his hair into watered black silk. He was looking at me as if I was his last chance of salvation.

My heart almost stopped beating.

'Jenny,' Con said hoarsely, before I could speak. 'I've changed my mind. I don't want you to leave. I never want you to leave.'

Tears blurred my vision and that stone was back in my throat, preventing me from speaking.

'You're in my heart,' he went on, dark eyes searching my face. 'You're part of me. You always have been. And I'm sorry I let you go. I'm sorry I sent you away. I truly thought that I was protecting you, but…you were right. You were right about all of it. Domingo did still have a hold on me. I wanted to believe what he said about me because…' Con took a deep, shuddering breath. 'I was afraid. Afraid of how deeply I felt about you. How deeply I loved you. I've loved you since you were eighteen.'

I blinked back the tears and my whole body was trembling with shock. And then, as that began to fade, reality began to sink in.

He *was* here. He really was. And he loved me.

Wordlessly, I reached for his hand and pulled him into the hall, out of the rain, shutting the door behind him.

He stood there, dripping on the threadbare carpet, not seeming at all bothered by how wet he was, staring only at me. His eyes burned with that dark fire I'd come to love so very much…the dark fire that lay at the heart of him.

'Val came to see me,' he said into the heavy silence, because my voice had stopped working. 'And he told me that I could choose to stay broken or I could choose to heal. And I…'

Con took a step towards me, his hands in fists at his sides, as if he was holding himself back from reaching for me.

'I didn't think it could be that simple. I didn't think I could just…choose it. And I thought of you, Jenny.'

His gaze intensified. 'I thought of you, and how honest you are with your emotions. So giving. You never hold anything back.'

He took another step, no ice at all in his fierce gaze now.

'But you always put what you need and what you want last, and that ends now. Someone needs to put you first, Jenny Grey, and I want that someone to be me. I want to be brave enough to heal, to let my father go to his grave, where he belongs, and I want to be strong enough to love you the way you should be loved. The way you *deserve* to be loved.'

My heart was a flower, opening up, spreading its petals wide to catch every drop of sunlight, reaching towards the light. Reaching for him.

I couldn't wait for him to close that last bit of distance, so I did. Going to him and putting my hands on his chest, not caring about his wet clothes. Not caring about anything but him.

'Then I'm yours,' I said simply, looking up at him, drinking in the sight of his beloved face. 'I've always been yours, Constantine Silvera.'

He took a sharp, ragged breath and lifted his hands, cupping my face between them. '*Dios*, I love you, my Jenny. I love you so much. I want to marry you. I want you to be my wife. And when our baby is born I want us to be a family. I want to make you happy.' His thumbs stroked over my cheekbones, the look on his face blazing bright. 'That's all I want. Just…to make you happy.'

I cried. I couldn't help it. The tears were streaming

down my cheeks, but this time they weren't from pain, but from happiness.

'I want that too,' I said thickly, and then, because words were too difficult, I went up on my toes and kissed him.

And he ignited.

Because Constantine Silvera had never been ice. He'd always been fire.

And so was I.

EPILOGUE

Constantine

THE DOOR TO the birthing suite opened and Valentin came out. He was carrying a small white bundle and looked completely shell-shocked.

I knew the feeling. Two years and three children later—a boy and twin girls—I still remembered the way it felt to hold your child in your arms for the first time. It was like being hit very hard over the back of the head.

Jenny launched herself out of the seat in the waiting room, where we'd been sitting, and flew over to him, cooing over my new nephew.

Our children were being looked after by the nanny. We'd been at a function to celebrate the launch of Jenny's new project—a children's charity I'd helped her set up, though only in a very limited capacity. Jenny was the most competent organiser I'd ever seen, and the charity was mostly her own work. I was just the backer.

Val had called me towards the end of the function, to let me know that Olivia had gone into labour. So we'd left the party early and come straight to the private hospital where Olivia was.

Jenny, still in her evening gown of soft, flowing golden silk, gave Val an enquiring look and then, when he nodded, gently took the baby into her arms.

She looked like a goddess in gold, cradling my nephew, and all I wanted was to take her home and worship her the way she deserved. And I couldn't deny that seeing her with a baby in her arms, made me want another of our own.

Laurent, our son, loved his sisters to distraction, but it would be nice if he could have a brother. I approved of brothers.

Mine, however, looked as if he needed some support, so I got up too, and went over to my dazed-looking twin, glancing down at the baby boy nestled in Jenny's arms.

'He's beautiful, Val,' she murmured, stroking his downy forehead. 'He's perfect.'

'Yes,' Val said, clearly unable to say anything else.

Jenny glanced up at him, then back at me, her dark eyes knowing. She eased the baby into Val's arms, then said, 'I'll go and see how Olivia is,' before slipping away into the birthing suite, allowing me some time alone with my brother.

She always knew what I needed, my Jenny, without me even having to say. Just as I knew what she needed too. Our connection was deep, strong, and as time went on it only got stronger.

'How do you do it?' Val asked, staring down at his newborn son with a fearful kind of awe written all over his face. 'How do you stand having your heart outside your chest like this?'

I put my hand on his shoulder and gave it a squeeze. We had walked a long, hard road, my brother and I, and it had taken time to rebuild our relationship. But now we were back where we'd first started. Together. Brothers for ever.

'Oh…' I said. 'You get used to it.'

I hadn't, not quite. But with Jenny's help I was getting there.

She'd put together the broken pieces of my soul and made me whole. And if sometimes the places where those pieces were joined ached a little, I'd learned to accept it. As she often told me, healing could be painful sometimes.

She was so full of wisdom, my Jenny.

I would love her until the end of time.

'You really get used to it?' Val asked with some disbelief.

'No,' I said, and smiled—another thing she'd taught me. 'You just learn to live with it.'

And I'd learned.

Love was a choice, and I chose it every day.

* * * * *

#4041 THE KING'S CHRISTMAS HEIR
The Stefanos Legacy
by Lynne Graham

When Lara rescued Gaetano from a blizzard, she never imagined she'd say "I do" to the man with no memory. Or, when the revelation that he's actually a future king rips their passionate marriage apart, that she'd be expecting a precious secret!

#4042 CINDERELLA'S SECRET BABY
Four Weddings and a Baby
by Dani Collins

Innocent Amelia's encounter with Hunter was unforgettable... and had life-changing consequences! After learning Hunter was engaged, she vowed to raise their daughter alone. But now, Amelia's secret is suddenly, scandalously exposed!

#4043 CLAIMED BY HER GREEK BOSS
by Kim Lawrence

Playboy CEO Ezio will do anything to save the deal of a lifetime. Even persuade his prim personal assistant, Matilda, to take a six-month assignment in Greece...as his convenient bride!

#4044 PREGNANT INNOCENT BEHIND THE VEIL
Scandalous Royal Weddings
by Michelle Smart

Her whole life, Princess Alessia has put the royal family first, until the night she let her desire for Gabriel reign supreme. Now she's pregnant! And to avoid a scandal, that duty demands a hasty royal wedding...

#4045 THEIR DESERT NIGHT OF SCANDAL
Brothers of the Desert
by Maya Blake

Twenty-four hours in the desert with Sheikh Tahir is more than Lauren bargained for when she came to ask for his help. Yet their inescapable intimacy empowers Lauren to lay bare the scandalous truth of their shared past—and her still-burning desire for Tahir...

#4046 AWAKENED BY THE WILD BILLIONAIRE
by Bella Mason

Colliding with a masked stranger at a ball sends shy Emma's pulse skyrocketing. And that's *before* he introduces himself as Alexander Hastings, the CEO with a wild side, which puts him way out of her league! Will Emma step out of the shadows and into the billionaire's penthouse?

#4047 THE MARRIAGE THAT MADE HER QUEEN
Behind the Palace Doors...
by Kali Anthony

To claim her crown, queen-to-be Lise must wed. The man she must turn to is Rafe, the self-made billionaire who once made her believe in love. He'll have to make her believe in it again for passion to be part of their future...

#4048 STRANDED WITH HIS RUNAWAY BRIDE
by Julieanne Howells

Surrendering her power to a man is unacceptable to Princess Violetta. Even *if* that man sets her alight with a single glance! But when Prince Leo tracks his runaway bride down and they are stranded together, he's not the enemy she first thought...

YOU CAN FIND MORE INFORMATION ON UPCOMING HARLEQUIN TITLES, FREE EXCERPTS AND MORE AT HARLEQUIN.COM.

HPCNMRB0822

*Colliding with a masked stranger at a ball sends
shy Emma's pulse skyrocketing. And that's before he
introduces himself as Alexander Hastings,
the CEO with a wild side, which puts him
way out of her league! Will Emma step out of the
shadows and into the billionaire's penthouse?*

*Read on for a sneak preview of Bella Mason's
debut story for Harlequin Presents,*
Awakened by the Wild Billionaire.

"Emma," Alex said, pinning her against the wall in a spectacularly graffitied alley, the walls an ever-changing work of art, when he could bear it no more. "I have to tell you. I really don't care about seeing the city. I just want to get you back in my bed."

He could barely believe that he wanted to take her back home. Sending her on her way was the smarter plan. But how smart was it really to deny himself? Emma knew the score. This wasn't about feelings or a relationship. It was just sex.

"Give me the weekend. I promise you won't regret it." His voice was low and rough. He could see in her eyes that she knew just how aroused he was, and with his body against hers, she could feel it.

"I want that too," she breathed.

"What I said before still stands. This doesn't change things."

"I know that." She grinned. "I don't want it to."

Don't miss
Awakened by the Wild Billionaire
available October 2022 wherever
Harlequin Presents books and ebooks are sold.

Harlequin.com